SALVAGED

AN URBAN FANTASY

WAYWARD MAGE BOOK THREE

ANN GIMPEL

CONTENTS

SALVAGED
WAYWARD MAGE BOOK THREE

An Urban Fantasy

By
Ann Gimpel

**Tumble off reality's edge into a dangerous world fueled
by lore and magic**

Copyright Page

BOOK DESCRIPTION: SALVAGED

Life used to be simple. I solved cases for mortals, earning myself a solid reputation as a crack detective. And I basked in the adoration of every animal, bird, and sea creature known to man—or sorcerer. My animal mage part is the same, but everything else has changed.

The last time I remember being happy was the day I married Blake. Since then, nothing has gone right. When he met me, I traveled beneath crossed stars. Jinxed is a kind term for the trouble that followed me.

He says we're stronger together, but I'm starting to doubt that. Some challenges are meant to be faced alone. Maybe I can fix the problems plaguing us. Maybe I can't, but I have to try.

And I must do it with my animal allies. Blake won't like any of this, which means I'll have to slip away when he's not paying attention. And I'll need to cover my tracks well to make sure he doesn't follow me.

He's my heart, my life, but if I don't leave him, he'll be doomed right along with me, and I refuse to let that happen.

BOOKS IN THE WAYWARD MAGE SERIES

Hands of Fate (a novella)
Jinxed
Hunted
Salvaged
Tiana

CHAPTER 1
ABRIA

"You're out of nuts," Hedrek hooted from the vicinity of my tiny kitchen.

I looked up from my computer screen. "So? Go hunting."

He's a magical owl, many times bigger than your average barn owl. And one of my self-appointed protectors. Maybe not exactly self-appointed. Arianrhod, Celtic goddess and virgin huntress, had tasked him with my safety. But that was a while ago. Neither of us had seen her since before I tackled the ley lines—and fixed them.

He flew into my study, perched on the edge of my desk, and announced, "It's not exactly safe for you to be here. I am not leaving."

I gave up on any catch-up for my private detective business. I hadn't taken a client for months, but people were still emailing. Gave me hope of resurrecting something viable.

Still, I couldn't concentrate with Hedrek nattering in one ear.

"What do you want to do?" I asked him.

"Return to Underhill. We're already much later than I promised Blake."

A sigh rattled from me. Once I'd been a free agent, totally on my own. Now I had a phalanx of babysitters. "Can you give me another half hour? Please." I moved from behind the monitor, smiled at the tawny owl with golden eyes, and added, "How about a few crackers? They're probably stale, but food is food."

"Meat?" A hopeful note fluttered beneath the one word.

"Look in the freezer."

He turned and flew back the way he'd come. I returned to my texts and emails. Electronics don't work in Underhill. Something about the energy of the Faery realm defeats the electromagnetic waves that power phones and tablets.

Blake hadn't been pleased about me returning to my home in Nairn. He'd insisted on sweeping the place to make certain it wasn't magically booby-trapped. It must have passed because he'd grudgingly allowed as to how I could access my home again.

A series of thumps from the kitchen suggested Hedrek had found what he sought. I hoped he didn't make too big a mess on my scarred wooden floor, but at least he'd be occupied for a while.

I hadn't spent five minutes with my correspondence before magical currents announced someone's imminent arrival. I shot to my feet, hands extended, defensive power balanced between them. If something bad happened here,

Blake would probably torch the place. At least then I could collect on the insurance.

I don't exactly need money anymore, not with all the wealth of Faery standing behind me as Blake's intended. But old habits die hard.

Hedrek blasted into the room in a whirlwind of feathers with something bloody hanging from his curved beak. Dropping his prize on my rug, where it was sure to leave a nasty stain, he said, "We're leaving."

"Shall we see who it is first?" I kept my voice even. Just because everyone else in my current universe was fussed up about my safety, I refused to live like that.

Hedrek landed in front of me, wings spread. "But I have to answer to Arianrhod," he protested. "And Blake."

A gateway formed near my front door, glowing blue-white. I'd know that magical signature anywhere. Leaping to my feet, I skirted the owl and hurried forward. "It's okay," I told Hedrek. "It's just Birgit."

With a flurry of huffing noises that weren't especially owl-like at all, he retreated to the glob he'd dropped. Too bad he didn't have the type of tongue that would effectively lick up the blood.

The gateway glowed brighter. I opened my arms as Birgit stepped through. About my height and wraith thin, she'd always reminded me of a raptor wearing human skin. Her hair was white and plaited into two thick braids that hung down her back. Ice-blue eyes regarded me from beneath white brows. Her face was all planes and angles with a sharp beak of a nose and a thin-lipped mouth.

Today, she was smiling as she walked into my embrace. "So good to see you," she announced before stepping back.

"You as well. How about a cup of tea?"

"I'd love one, but don't you have things to do? It's your wedding day, child."

I made a face. "Gah. Don't remind me. It's why I'm here. I had to get out of Underhill. Everyone was driving me nuts with all the preparations. And Blake is so nervous, he may back out at the last minute."

"That will never happen," Birgit said, her words steeped in conviction.

We walked into the kitchen with Hedrek trailing behind us. Good thing since he'd left the freezer door wide open with an assortment of packages of frozen meat strewn across the floor. I bent to pick them up.

"Not done yet," he croaked.

A staunch meow preceded a hefty black tomcat jumping out of somewhere in Birgit's deep-green robe. He landed on the floor and rolled one of the packages over with a paw before turning to the owl. "Mind if we share?" Jethro purred fetchingly.

Tough to refuse him anything when he purred like that. He's a Sidhe seer who spends most of him time in cat form. He and Birgit go back a long way.

I put the kettle on. Hedrek picked up one of the frozen packets and pushed it Jethro's way. Rearing back on his haunches, the cat mimed a bow before ripping paper off the frozen whatever it was.

"So how are you feeling?" Birgit inquired once I'd poured

boiling water over a combination of mint, anise, and rosemary.

"About?"

She pursed her lips into a thin line. "Don't be disingenuous with me, dearie."

Busted.

"Wasn't trying to be. Not on purpose, anyway," I replied. "I love Blake, but he comes with so much baggage."

She cackled. "Oh. You mean the rest of the Sidhe?"

I nodded. "And his responsibility to them."

"Is it you who's thinking about backing out?"

Her question caught me where I live. I considered my answer carefully. "No. Not exactly. He and I are meant to be together, but trouble lies ahead. A lot of it. I'd prefer if he were safe, and I'll be damned if I implicate the Sidhe in my problems."

Birgit drew her white brows together. "But you fixed the ley lines. Are other mages still after you?"

I set my cup down and pinched the bridge of my nose between a thumb and forefinger before meeting her gaze. "Not sure who's after me, but someone is."

She spun a hand. "Tell me."

"Nothing specific. Not really, but I keep having these fucking dreams where I'm riding at the head of an army. It's me and Becca and this golden stag, and—"

"Whoa. A stag, you say?" At my nod, she went on. "You're dreaming of the Hunt, child."

My eyes widened. "The Wild Hunt? But that's straight out of Norse mythology."

"Your point?" Birgit's blue gaze drilled into me.

I shrugged. "Not my pantheon."

"If you're dreaming about the stag, it certainly is." She leaned against the back of her chair. "Once the wedding is past, we need to investigate. I know Odin, and—"

"Blake isn't going to like this," I muttered.

"'Tisn't for him to judge," she said tartly. "But you might hold off on telling him until after the ceremony."

"He already knows," I said dully. "And he didn't breathe a word about the Norse gods."

Her rugged features mirrored confusion. "But surely he must know the significance of the stag. Herne led the original Hunt—before Odin took over. Never was sure what became of the horned god."

I got to my feet and ferried our mugs to the sink. Since I was close to the cold box, I closed the freezer door. It appeared all the frozen meat was well on its way down furred and feathered gullets. I'd clear away the wrappings later.

"We should go back," I muttered.

"About time." Hedrek looked up from his meal.

"Where's your dress?" Birgit asked.

"It's a tunic and pants. Everything is in Underhill."

She was on her feet. Coming close, she wrapped her arms around me. "It will be better than you believe."

"What will be?" My voice was muffled against her shoulder.

"Why your future. Yours and Blake's. Jethro's seen snatches of it."

A deep purr corroborated her statement.

Part of me was still considering simply vanishing, but it

would break Blake's heart. Unfortunately, it would shatter mine as well. No way out but through, which isn't how most gals approach their wedding day.

I left the cups in the sink and turned off my computer. By the time I was done, Birgit was standing by the remnants of her portal with Jethro in her arms and Hedrek next to her. I joined them, and we walked through the witch's gateway into Underhill near the council chamber.

"Neat trick," I told her.

"Bests teleporting for short trips," she agreed.

Short trips, eh? "I had no idea my place in Nairn was anywhere near Underhill," I mumbled.

"It wasn't, but Blake fixed that."

I resisted rolling my eyes. Of course, he would have.

"I'll see you later today," Hedrek informed me and squeezed through Birgit's portal just as it was closing. He had magic aplenty to bend it to his will.

"You're not ready yet." Breanne's tone held censure as she hustled toward us. Tall and broad, were it not for breasts, she'd have been built like a linebacker.

"I have time," I protested.

"Precious little," she retorted and made shooing motions as if I were a chicken or something.

I took a good look at her. Her usual battle axe was absent, and she was wearing something decidedly feminine for her: a cream-colored robe trimmed in lace and sashed in deep blue. White hair curled around her face, and her grey eyes sparked with unusual excitement.

"Hurry." She gave me a little shove.

"Get dressed," Birgit suggested. "Breanne and I can catch up."

A reprieve! I didn't wait around but hustled to the rooms I share with Blake. I hadn't expected him to be there, and he wasn't. The door opened obligingly as soon as I got close to it. That was something new.

Someone had laid my finery out on a low table near the bed. I shucked my pants and sweatshirt, stood under the shower for a few moments, and was drying off when I heard Blake's footsteps.

He poked his head into the steamy bathroom. Every time I look at him, my heart stutters and breath catches in my throat. I may fuss and fume about how he hovers over me, but he is the most breathtaking man I've ever laid eyes on. Today, in his wedding garments, he was even more stunning.

If it were even possible.

All Sidhe carry an otherworldly beauty; he was no exception with his sculpted facial structure and gorgeous black wings with jewel-toned inserts. Silky black hair brushed his collarbones. Dark eyes held a hypnotic inner fire. A shred taller than me, his shoulders are broad. Slim hips, long legs, and an athlete's build completed the picture.

The warmth from his smile sank into my soul. "There you are." His voice was deep, rich, melodic. "I'd been wondering if you changed your mind."

I hung the towel over a hook and walked into his open arms. The silk of his emerald-green robe tantalized my naked flesh. He hugged me and nuzzled my neck. I wrapped my arms around him, luxuriating in the play of bone and muscle beneath my fingertips.

The swell of his erection butted into my belly. I reached between us to cup him in a hand. "Do we have time?"

He disentangled us, one from the other. "Unfortunately, no, my love."

I gave his cock one more squeeze before letting go. "Too bad."

"Hang onto that thought. There's always after the ceremony. When everyone expects us to disappear."

I felt his gaze on me as I pulled a pair of soft brown linen trousers over my legs. A white long-sleeved tunic hand embroidered with runes followed. I rustled through my jewelry box and withdrew a five-carat square-cut emerald suspended from a golden chain. Blake fastened it around my neck.

My usual boots or running shoes wouldn't do at all. Someone had placed a pair of strappy silver sandals next to the bed. I slid them on and buckled them.

"You never answered me," Blake said.

I'd moved on to brushing out my long hair. "About what?"

"Second thoughts?"

My cheeks warmed, a dead giveaway that meant I couldn't twist the truth. I looked up from where I perched on the edge of the bed. "Of course, I considered dropping out of sight. Trouble follows me wherever I go. I'm not happy about involving you or your people."

"You can't know the future. Besides, if the Sidhe were at

war—and technically, we still are with our Cait cousins—you wouldn't have abandoned me."

Ouch. Point taken.

I got to my feet and walked to where he waited for me near the door. "I do love you, Blake. Never doubt it."

He tucked my hand between both of his. "I don't. We're stronger together, Abria. I waited a long time for you." His smile drilled through all my reservations. "You are the most beautiful, most fetching, unbelievably gorgeous woman I've ever known."

I grinned. "Admit it. You love me for my rapier-sharp wit and inquiring mind."

"Those too." He let go and offered his arm. "Shall we?"

I nodded, and the heady scents of the natural world bombarded me as he transported us to a deserted stretch of beach off the highway north of Nairn. I'd first met Cailleach here, and we'd selected it as a perfect spot for our nuptials since it meant the mer-people, seals, walruses, and fish could join all the other animals and share our joy.

We emerged in a shower of white sparks. Everyone was already assembled; cheers rose from Sidhe throats. Hundreds of animals, birds, and sea creatures surged forward, surrounding us with hoots, caws, honks, purrs, squeals, and yips.

Arianrhod, Ceridwen, and Cailleach waited on the beach with a fire burning between them. A triumvirate of crones and their holy flames.

We walked forward until we stood a meter away facing them with the fire between us.

Birgit flanked me on my right side with Jethro strutting next to her.

Kirwan stood next to Blake.

I've never attended a Sidhe wedding. Why would I have? In truth, I can count the weddings I've been part of through my 700 plus years on the fingers of one hand.

Chanting rose from the goddesses, their music creating runes in the gusty marine air. For once, the sun was out, but it didn't surprise me. Power untold was arrayed in front of us. Surely, they could hold back Scotland's notoriously bleak weather for a short while.

Blake vowed all the things a groom usually does, his words binding him with blood and magic. I promised him everything in return, mirroring his words. Cailleach made long cuts in our forearms. Where our blood joined, it created multihued streamers that floated around us before being absorbed by the fire.

So that was why it was there.

Blood gives our enemies power over us. The goddesses weren't taking any chances. If darkness stalked this beach once we were gone, there'd be naught to harvest.

It might have been the chanting or the singing or the runes or the blood, but the last of my reservations fell away. I couldn't imagine my life without Blake. And then he was kissing me, and people were yelling bawdy suggestions and mobbing us. Everyone wanted a kiss or a hug or a word.

The wound on my arm closed as if it had never been there. Likewise, the rent in my tunic vanished.

Animals wormed their way through the Sidhe, determined

to wish me, their queen, well. Equally determined to thank each and every one of them, I pushed through the crowed and took up a spot on a large flat rock. At some point, Blake joined me.

The sun was edging toward the western horizon when the last of my retinue faded away. Someone placed goblets of mead into our hands and toasted our marriage. We repaired to caves set into the cliffs where tables teemed with delicacies.

Blake tapped my shoulder. "It's been five minutes," he said around a mouthful of something-or-other.

"Since?" I chewed and swallowed the last of a piece of a quiche-like treat.

"Anyone's come over," he clarified. "I don't want to tear you away from your wedding, but we could leave anytime."

"You're about as subtle as a steam engine, bud." I arched both brows. "Where are we going?"

"It's a surprise."

I clapped my hands together, feeling young and carefree. It wouldn't last, so I was determined to enjoy it while I could. "A honeymoon?"

"Nothing that elaborate, but I did carve out a private spot for us outside of Underhill."

"Oooh. Where?"

In answer, he scooped me into his arms and ignited a travel spell he must have had at the ready. When it cleared, we were in an elaborate, old-fashioned bedchamber in what appeared to be a castle.

He put me down, and I strode to expansive windows overlooking lush grounds. Several pairs of swans swam this way and that on a lake two stories below.

Blake wrapped his arms around me from behind. "Do you like it?"

I turned and hugged him. "I love it."

"Good." He beamed at me. "Sometimes my other life as Earl of Galloway comes in handy. This is Castle Douglas. I rented the whole thing for a few days. Just for us."

I nestled against him. "We could have gone back to Underhill."

He stroked my hair. "We could have, but I wanted something special. And somewhere we'd be left alone."

Love for the man in my arms surged, filling me with such strong emotions I could scarcely contain them. I'm sure they spilled out this way and that as Blake settled his mouth over mine.

Lost in the power whirling around us, I opened my mouth to his questing tongue.

Sex is the easy part, an inner voice warned. I shushed it and went to work divesting my brand new husband of his clothing.

CHAPTER 2

BLAKE

I cradled Abria against me as she slept, keeping both my arms and wings wrapped around her. We'd made love for hours, waking to select treats from room service, showering, and falling back into bed. For the first time since our first time in her flat, I was sated.

The musk of our lovemaking permeated the room. Elegant and traditional with its stone hearth and high, coved ceilings, it was perfect for our initial days as a mated couple. I tugged a duvet over the top of us. These old castles are romantic, but they never were very warm despite having fireplaces in every room.

Abria's long red hair caught on the edge of the comforter. I smoothed it aside and drank her in. Men would have fought wars over magnificence such as hers. In olden times, they did. She's as tall as me, which is slightly over six feet, with thick curls that cascade well below her waist. Green eyes are tilted at the corners, and sometimes she looks like a mischievous cat. Unlike many redheads, her skin isn't fair but holds notes of pink and copper. The mounds of her breasts were squished against my chest. One long, shapely leg was tossed over my hip. I adore looking at her, studying her pronounced cheekbones, rounded chin, and high forehead. Long lashes brushed her cheeks. Her beauty holds an exotic charm, and she's striking enough to turn heads wherever she travels.

But the best part is she's unaware of her impact on others and content to surround herself with the animals who adore her.

Abria murmured in her sleep. I built a small spell to ensure she rested, and then shut my eyes as well. The wedding had been an indulgence, but after everything we'd lived through, we deserved a small window of peace. I'd been surprised by the turnout. I'd expected all manner of bird, beast, and fish, but Sidhe I hadn't seen in millennia had come too. A few actually left the *Dreaming* to attend.

No doubt, they'd given up on me, their regent, ever joining his life to anyone's. Mages rarely formalize matings. When you live forever, tastes can change, and it's far simpler to remain with the love interest *du jour* until ardor wanes. Not that I'd ever even so much as set up housekeeping with another—until Abria.

Once I met her, she'd occupied every waking thought.

Finally, finally, she was mine. If I had my way, we'd never be separated.

Aye, mate. Get your head on straight.

She wasn't Sidhe, not one of my subjects, and not especially biddable under the best of circumstances. Her independence was one of the things I fell in love with. Good thing since it wasn't likely to change.

"You're awake," she mumbled, her words saturated with drowsiness.

She opened her eyes and gazed at me. For once, worry didn't stain her brow or crinkle the skin around her eyes.

"Just enjoying looking at you," I said.

"Flattery will get you everywhere." She smiled. It began in her eyes before spreading to her mouth. "I could remain here for hours, days, weeks ordering from room service, making love, and then doing it all over again."

"I can extend our reservation."

Something bittersweet dimmed her smile. "Maybe we could return for our anniversaries." She wound her arms around me and stroked the place where my wings extend from my shoulders.

"How about just one more day?" I really did not want to leave. Once we were back in Underhill, a million details would vie for my attention.

She nestled into the hollow of my collarbone and licked my neck. It got me going all over again. As if it hadn't been involved in almost nonstop action for the better part of forty-eight hours, my cock thickened, pressing into her belly.

"I know this song," she murmured, her voice muffled against my flesh. "It's the same one that caught us up when we met. One day leads to another and before we know it, months have flown past. You can't do that to your people. Not again."

I winced. My protracted absences had come at inopportune times for the Sidhe. In all fairness, my original dalliance with Abria had been but one of many times I hadn't been accessible—to anyone. I'd vowed to be more present, to serve as the regent the Sidhe had appointed me to be. My leadership role was in name only most of the time, but when shit got rolling, my people needed someone to cut through interminable discussions and pick a path for us.

I shut off my thoughts and kissed Abria, long, slow, lazy, enjoying the sensation of her lips against mine. No matter how often we made love, each time could have been our first all over again.

"This isn't only about me," I said between kisses.

A corner of her mouth curled downward. "Never could skate much past you."

Reaching between us, she took me in her hand teasing as she ran a fingertip the length of my shaft. "Once more," she murmured, "but then there are things we must discuss before we leave here."

Her tone sounded alarm bells deep in my mind. Whatever it was, I wanted to know now, but I never could refuse her anything. When she pushed one of my shoulders flat against the plush mattress and straddled me, I shoved everything else aside.

Her vulva spread across my cock, encasing it with heat. Reaching for her breasts, I pinched the nipples into peaks. She made a small mewing noise that got me hotter than hell and rotated her hips from side to side. Bending, she settled her mouth atop mine and plunged her tongue deep.

Heat and need engulfed me. I bit her tongue and then traded, shoving mine into her open mouth. Our teeth crashed together; she moaned low in the back of her throat and rubbed the seat of her sensation against my more-than-ready member.

I pried my hands out from between our bodies and ran my nails down the silken skin of her back. I could almost feel goosebumps follow the path of my touch. When I got to her ass, I kneaded the smooth, creamy globes. She thrust her hips against my belly. My cock was on fire with needing to be inside her.

But once I entered her, this would be over far too soon. I wanted her, and the joy we wrung from one another's bodies, far more than I wanted to return to whatever problems had cropped up during our absence.

They couldn't be too bad, I lied to myself. Someone would have ferreted me out if I were needed. Except, they couldn't. Not easily, anyway. I hadn't told a soul where we'd be, and I'd concealed our travel path as well as I could. Arianrhod or Ceridwen could locate us. Cailleach, too. but I felt certain the task was beyond the other Sidhe.

Abria ripped her lips from mine. "I'm here," she announced. "Your mind is a long way off."

"Not that far," I murmured. Placing my hands on her hips, I lifted her easily, swung her to the side, and laid her on her back. Her legs fell open, and I knelt between them. Spiky red curls surrounded her engorged sex. It was my goal, but I started with her flat stomach, kissing from one pronounced hipbone to the next and back again.

Breathing, licking, biting, kissing, I worked my way down to her sex. For a time I hovered over the delicious bit of flesh just breathing heat onto it. She grabbed my head and pushed downward while raising her hips to meet my tongue.

I lifted my head. "Hussy."

"You like your women loose; admit it." She bucked her hips again.

"Don't know about 'my women,' but I adore you just the way you are."

"Talk is cheap. Show me." A wanton grin painted her face. Splotches of color highlighted both cheeks.

I quit teasing and licked around and around her clit before taking the whole thing into my mouth and sucking hard. Sliding a hand between her legs, I shoved two fingers into her vault. I'd meant to draw this out, but that never worked for us. Between pants and squeals and moans, she came once and then again. I've always loved how responsive she is.

I swallowed her juices and licked her thighs. Before I could recapture her clit, she jackknifed her body from under mine, and twisted until she knelt, ass in the air. The sight of her sex on display was always a treat. And it was new every time, as if I'd never seen her like this before.

The invitation was obvious. I moved behind her, grasped her hips, and sank into her. Being surrounded by her electric energy drove everything else from my mind. We were everything, the entire universe. Nothing beyond our bodies had ever existed. Only Abria and me and the erotic dance our bodies created.

I wove power around us to heighten our pleasure. Pale streamers fluttered, stroking us in strategic spots. My wings spread to the sides. I withdrew, teased the opening to her body by moving my cock in tiny circles before sinking back inside the liquid heat of her.

She tightened around me. I twitched back. For a time we traded the smallest of motions while passion built. Colors danced around us, courtesy of the streamers. I set two to circle her nipples. Reaching around I settled a hand over her sex and rubbed her slick nub.

We'd played this game before. It was a contest to see who broke first and started to move.

"Damn you," she cried and butted her hips upward.

It was exactly what I'd been waiting for, and hoping to hell I didn't come before I'd gotten a few more thrusts in. That had happened before too.

I steadied her hips with one hand and curled a wing over the other side. Rubbing her with the other hand, I withdrew, but not all the way. Abria writhed beneath me. Tension in her vault translated to my cock buried in her body.

Suddenly, I was done playing, done teasing. My body developed a mind of its own, and I fucked her hard and fast. I felt her release, tried to hang on, and failed. I could have employed magic, but I craved the sensation of orgasm more. Nothing was more wonderful than coming inside Abria.

Semen bubbled from my balls, exiting in long lazy jets. A guttural roar made me hope the castle's old walls were thick enough to deaden sound. I came for a long time. My vision hazed over, and I was above the bed watching us and sunk deep into rut at the same time.

She collapsed onto her belly with me on top of her.

"This just keeps getting better," I murmured when I was capable of speech.

"Practice makes perfect," she purred.

"Just think where we'll be at after a couple of centuries," I joked back.

"By then, we'll have half a dozen kids under foot. They have a way of putting a damper on amorous adventures."

Her words got my attention. I extracted myself from her body, turned us on our sides, and asked, "Did you mean that?"

"Which part?" Her heavy-lidded gaze was saturated with spent lust.

"The children part."

Her eyes widened. "Oh, yeah. We never actually talked about that. Do you want children?"

It wasn't a trick question. Why was it so hard to answer?

She started to say either way was all right, but I waved her to silence. "I've never put much thought into it, but yes, I do want children with you. Maybe we'll have a stable of little animal mages."

Abria grinned. "We'll see. I have no idea if I can even bear children, but we'll find out."

I draped a wing over her. "That we will, but not until we're not dealing with enemies from all sides."

Breath huffed from her; her gaze was still glued to mine. "Remember when I told you about the dream with Becca and the stag?"

I rustled through my memory banks. "Aye. I do. Why?"

She closed her teeth over her lower lip. "Why didn't you tell me what the stag symbolized?"

I reconstructed the dream but couldn't come up with

anything I hadn't said at the time. "Probably because I have no idea."

Abria was still staring me down. "That's odd because Birgit knew right away."

I started to mutter, bully for her, but zipped it. She and Abria were close friends. "What did she say about the stag that caught your attention?"

"It symbolizes the Wild Hunt. I have to find him to make sense of what comes next."

The pleasant haze from our lovemaking shattered. I tightened my grip on Abria. "Him as in Odin?"

A small shrug. "Whatever it takes, but probably the stag. From everything I've read, Odin would never grant an interview to anyone as low on the totem pole as me."

"I'm coming with you."

She shook her head. "Maybe. Let's see what it looks like back in Underhill. You may be needed there."

I resisted an urge to rocket to my feet and shake a finger at her while stating she was not going into the Norse realms by herself.

"I wouldn't go by myself, silly," she said.

"Get out of my head." It was petty of me, but this was one time I did not want her privy to my thoughts.

"I'll leave you to your privacy when you leave me to mine."

Ouch. I gave it a good-faith effort but couldn't manage to utter the words, "Fair is fair."

She scootched out of my embrace and rolled to a sit. "I had a feeling you'd react this way—"

"I am not reacting." Defensiveness speared me.

Compared with what I wanted to do and say, I was actually behaving rather well.

"Ooooh. Is this our first married fight?"

Her smile was infectious. "Maybe half our first married fight," I admitted and laughed.

"Better." She got to her feet and offered me a hand. "This has been lovely, Blake. Amazing. Perfect. But it's time we went home."

I grasped her hand and stood. "Shower first?"

"Sure, but no monkey business." She strode toward the open bathroom door.

"No promises," I called after her and picked up our various discarded garments. We'd need them once we were clean.

The sound of running water drew me into the bathroom. Clouds of steam wafted out the door. I stepped into them, my mind busy recalling everything I knew about Odin, Thor, and the rest of the crew who lived in Valhalla.

Something didn't quite compute, though. Herne had led the first Wild Hunt, but then Odin took over. To the best of my knowledge, he still ran the show. No one—including me —had any idea what had happened to Herne these past few centuries. Yet, Abria was dreaming of him, not Odin.

I'd get to the bottom of this somehow. And I'd try to keep Abria out of Asgard.

May as well hold back the tides, mate, an inner voice snarked.

I'd have silenced it, except, in this case, it spoke true.

CHAPTER 3
ABRIA

Trapped between disappointment and resignation, I joined Blake's travel spell to return us to Underhill. Part of me had sort of hoped he'd put up more of a fuss about leaving the charming castle where we'd honeymooned. Another part was relieved our discussion hadn't turned into a rip-roaring argument.

The resignation part was because it was time to pick up the reins and face whatever lay ahead.

A change had come over Blake when I mentioned the Hunt. He'd been telling the truth when he claimed not to have made the connection between it and the stag in my dreams.

Since Birgit picked up on it right away, I wondered why the association hadn't immediately occurred to him as well. Did he and Odin have unpleasant history? It seemed likely. Now wasn't the time to ask, though.

I'd removed myself from Blake's mind, but I knew he

was trying out arguments to keep me from leaving Underhill on my own. Not that I'd be alone. Animals would accompany me, but none of it would matter to him. After a few times when I'd been captured, I'm sure he was loathe to allow me out of his sight.

Except that approach would never work.

I might be his mate, but I would never be his prisoner. I winced. Harsh words. Good thing he wasn't trolling through my head at the moment. At least, I hoped he wasn't.

The familiar smell of Underhill surrounded me. Damp evergreens, salty ocean, growing plants. I was starting to accept it as my home too. Perhaps a mistake before the Sidhe accepted me. No other magic wielder except Blake ever has, so why would they?

Not quite true, an inner voice reminded me. And it wasn't. Birgit and Jethro were friends. So was Cailleach, sort of. Arianrhod had come around to a point where she tolerated me. The Sidhe might welcome me into their ranks eventually.

It wasn't my main concern.

When Blake's spell retreated, we stood in his sitting room still garbed in our wedding finery. Neither of us had thought to bring a change of clothes. Guess we'd known we'd never leave the hotel suite.

His arms still circled me. "I had some of your things moved from your flat in Nairn," he said. "They're in the teak armoire in the bedchamber."

"Thank you." I skipped the part about feeling violated anyone had culled through my garments. I could have done that, but he'd wanted me to feel at home right away. Besides, he'd rightly intuited I wouldn't have time.

He placed a hand on each shoulder. "Once I've changed, I need to check in with the council. You're welcome to accompany me."

I shook my head. "You need private time with your people."

"Promise me you'll be here when I get back."

Oh-oh. It was starting.

"I can't do that," I said not wanting to lie to him.

"All right." His hands tightened on my shoulders. "At least promise you won't run off to Valhalla half-cocked."

"How about if I run off fully cocked?" I tried for a jaunty grin.

He stopped shy of shaking me, but he wanted to. "Damn it, Abria. This isn't funny. Have you ever been to the Norse realm?"

I shook my head again.

"Thought so. 'Tisn't straightforward. At all. Yggdrasil guards every entry. You cannot sneak past the One Tree. And if it decides you have no business there, it ejects you."

"So? I'd just try again."

He smiled grimly. "I think not. It's damnably disagreeable."

"Has it happened to you?"

"Aye. More than once." Blake hesitated. "Make no mistake. Odin is a bastard. He hobnobs with the dead. My observation is he has little use for the living. If you manage to make it past Yggdrasil, frost giants live in Jotenheim. Except they don't remain there, and they eat whatever crosses their path. Hel and her serpents pose another problem."

"Serpents I can handle."

"I'm the first to admire your ability, but it may not hold sway over those two."

I took a measured breath. Blake wouldn't quit hovering until he extracted a promise from me. "Today, I will remain close. Not necessarily in Underhill, but I won't leave Earth."

The tense line of his shoulders relaxed; so did his grip on me. "Thank you, Abria."

"Don't get carried away," I warned him. "Tomorrow will be another story. I have to find out more about the stag, about why he's in my dreams almost every night. His appearance must be important."

Blake kissed my forehead before walking toward the bedchamber. "Maybe the Hunt will come to you. Except now Odin heads it up. Not sure what happened to Herne."

The Hunt finding me wasn't an option I'd considered, mostly since I'd never run into them before. Never even seen a trace in the night skies. Unlike many of the better-known deities, I hadn't given the Hunt a single, solitary thought.

Until now.

The sounds of rustling came from the bedroom. I followed them, still smitten enough to crave the sight of Blake's naked form. Except I was too late. He'd dressed in record time, trading his ceremonial duds for a beige robe sashed in deep green.

The council must be breathing down his neck, but he hadn't mentioned a word about it.

He plucked a leatherbound book from off a shelf. "See you later, darling. Dinner here around seven?"

"What time is it now?" We'd left Castle Douglas at noon, but time flows differently in Underhill.

"Just past three in the afternoon." He angled his head to one side. "Are you planning to change?"

Vintage Blake. Not so different from me. "Yeah, but after you leave."

"Tease."

I unbuttoned the top two fastenings on my tunic, opening the top to between my breasts, and sashayed toward him, hips swaying provocatively. "You want teasing?"

"Always, so long as it's from you."

I reached for the next button in line. He swooped past, palmed a breast, and hurried toward the doorway. "Hold that pose, darling. For later."

Laughing, I waited until I heard the outer door open and shut before I made my way to the teak armoire to take stock of what was here. Not everything, but enough.

I slithered out of my clothes, placing the tunic and pants on a hanger. I'd given up on undergarments long since, but I found a sturdy pair of trousers and a woolen shirt. The only thing I was missing was boots, but I'd left a pair here. A cursory search turned them up on the floor of the armoire.

Someone was organized.

Very organized. My bent was to leave clothing in piles or stacked on top of each other on hooks in my messy closet.

I had a few hours. Maybe Underhill's library was a good place to start. Blake kept a small collection in his rooms, but

I wanted the mother lode. I could learn about Odin and his Hunt, so I'd be better prepared. I stepped outside Blake's rooms and looked up and down passageways that extended to infinity. Where was the library?

For a time, I wandered this way and that, but then I wised up and dialed in my psychic senses. Old vellum has a particular feel about it. So does magic, and many of the books and scrolls were spelled to defeat casual exploration.

Sure enough, a path lit before me. At its end, a cavernous room opened with shelving running four meters up every wall. I felt a zing as I walked inside, no doubt a built-in warding device. Not that anyone could get this deep into Underhill without being detected, but this chamber held a priceless—and irreplaceable—collection of knowledge. The Sidhe weren't taking any chances.

I scanned the lower rows of titles. Many were in languages I didn't read, which didn't bode well for being able to translate whatever lay within. I made a single transit of the shelves I could reach. If there was a card catalog system, it was far from obvious.

"Guess if you have to ask, you don't deserve to know," I muttered.

"Looking for anything special?" was preceded by Breanne's bulk and her heavy tread.

Should I tell her? Not as if it were a secret, or it wouldn't be once I left in search of my stag.

"Abria?" She joined me in front of a bank of scrolls so old they smelled moldy.

"I'm looking for material on the Wild Hunt," I told her.

White brows shot up. "Really. Why?"

Damn the Sidhe. Nothing was ever simple. I faced her, noticing her battle axe was back in place, strapped across her back. She'd jettisoned it for the wedding. "Because I've been dreaming about a golden stag," I told her.

Her eyebrows edged up another notch. "Really? For how long?"

Does it matter? I bit my tongue and answered, "Maybe a month. Birgit believes it's a signpost for my next moves."

"Mmph. Does Blake know?"

"Of course." I left it at that. No reason to mention his reaction.

The rigid set of her shoulders relaxed. "I don't believe Herne leads the Hunt any longer, but let me teach you how to access knowledge. Hold an image in your mind of what you want to know. Like this."

Power circled my mind as she drew me into her spell. Visions of a broad-shouldered one-eyed man with steel gray hair that fell halfway down his back in rows of braids filled my mind. He rode an eight-legged horse, and a phalanx of dead warriors followed him.

Visible motes of golden light formed a circle that grew until it encompassed the oblong room. One by one, books and scrolls floated to a long central table. Breanne barked a word. The spell frittered to wisps.

She dusted thick-fingered hands together. "Should be enough to get you started," she said brusquely and stomped out of the library.

Talk about an understatement. If I sat here for two weeks, I'd never work my way through all this material. First, I sorted everything into languages I could read versus ones that would require either magic or a translator. Next I conjured a pot of herbal tea and settled in to read.

I'm sure I've mentioned there are no day-night cycles in Underhill. Makes it tough to estimate the passage of time. I found paper and pencils in a drawer from a desk that sat in one corner. From time to time I jotted down notes as the structure of Odin's realm became more real for me. Nine worlds guarded by Yggdrasil, the One Tree.

The stag likely lived with the Frost Giants or with Hel, or perhaps in Asgard. If it was even real. None of the depictions I found of the Hunt included a stag. Only Odin and his long-dead band of bawdy warriors. Could Birgit have been mistaken?

I was puzzling over that when Blake's distinctive foot-steps brought my head up. I stood and walked to meet him as he came through the door.

"Good choice of activities." He swept an arm to encom-pass the cluttered table. "Did you learn much?"

"Yes and no." I plopped back into my chair.

He drew one up next to me and sat. "Ready for supper?"

"In a little bit." Snatching a scroll, I shoved it between us. "Look at this part please."

When he glanced up, he said, "What did you want to know?"

"Every description of the Hunt reads a lot like this. Where does the stag come in?"

He nodded, got back to his feet, and walked the length of the table turning titles so he could read them. Not finding what he sought, he spread his wings, flew to an upper shelf, and selected a book and a scroll. Once he returned, he said, "These are what you're looking for."

I opened the book and shook my head. "Can't read this one."

Blake waved a hand over it. The script changed to Gaelic. "Better?" he inquired.

"Wish I could do that."

"You can. Just—"

I held up a hand. "One thing at a time. Teach me later."

The book's pages riffled until it fell open. Another handy trick. An illustration of the Hunt spanned both pages. Rather than the usual cast of characters, this version of Odin's nighttime scavengers included my stag, a murder of crows, two eagles, and an owl not unlike Hedrek.

Was it Hedrek? Good question. If so, it argued he knew the stag.

I read the accompanying text, but it didn't say much other than introducing Odin, Thor, Valhalla, and Asgard. For once, Blake was quiet.

"Why does this book carry such a divergent description?" I asked.

"It's much older."

Okay, still doesn't tell me much. "Did the Hunt change?" I probed.

Blake shook his head. "Most Pantheon-related matters are way above my pay grade. So the short answer is I don't exactly know."

"Are all these other sources wrong?" I persisted.

"Again, I'm not sure."

I flipped the pages back to where I'd begun and stabbed a finger at the owl. "Looks like Hedrek."

"It does, indeed. You might ask him."

"He's old, huh?"

Blake grunted what was probably assent.

I propped my head on a hand. Could it be that simple? If Hedrek held the answers I sought, it would save me oodles of trouble, maybe keep me out of Asgard or Valhalla or wherever the hell Odin hung out.

After closing the book, I rubbed my eyes. They were tired, a dead giveaway I'd been at this longer than I thought. When I opened them, I asked, "Have you ever had a run-in with Odin?"

"You might call it that. I'm below his elevated status, and he made it abundantly clear."

"Want to tell me what happened?"

A sigh rattled from him. "May as well since you'll keep after me until I do."

"I'm not that awful," I protested.

"Persistence isn't a bad thing." He paused before going on. "Long ago, when I wasn't much more than a youth, I stumbled across one of Yggdrasill's roots. It was the one belonging to Midgard."

"That's one of the Nine Worlds specific to mortals, isn't it?"

Blake nodded. "The magical world is supposed to be invisible to humans, yet this root had definitely intruded to such an extent people not only noticed, but built a shrine around it. Remember, this was hundreds of years ago when humans still believed in magic and miracles.

"I figured Odin should know because the root's presence broke our mutual covenant, the one that instructed us to remain out of sight."

"Not all of us followed that precept," I murmured. "The Siren call of adulation from mortals ran strong. It strengthened our power." I blew out a breath. "Nothing like collecting offerings, not that anyone ever made them for me."

"Animals did," Blake said softly.

Chagrin speared me. "I wasn't discounting them." Hell no, I wasn't. In many ways, my animal honor guard trumped anything humans could have ginned up.

"Anyway," Blake went on, "I made my way from the miscreant root up the One Tree until I crossed Bifrost, the bridge into Asgard. Things grew...interesting after that. First Frost Giants chased me until I jumped back onto the bridge. It's forbidden to them. I waited for a long while before trying again. This time, I snuck through Asgard well-warded and made my way to the golden streets near Valhalla.

"Huginn and Muninn discovered me. A gilded cage dropped over my ward, which they must have seen straight through. Next thing I knew, they grabbed the cage and flew me into the palace."

"Odin's ravens," I mumbled.

"Aye. Although, why they stick with him is beyond me. He paced and fumed and screamed. He threatened to feed me to his dead warriors. Or maybe it was the living ones. He wasn't all that articulate. When he finally ran down, I explained who I was and why I was there."

"Somehow I have a feeling it didn't exactly fix anything," I cut in.

"It didn't. Only earned me a fresh round of admonitions where he said he'd run his affairs as he saw fit. I'd been caged the whole time. It shattered around me, and a huge gust of wind picked me up and carried me back to where I'd begun."

Blake shook himself from head to foot to rid himself of the memory before adding. "When I went to look for the root, it was gone."

"So he did listen," I ventured.

"Maybe. I didn't return to have a chat about it. I have seen the Hunt a few times, though. It was always comprised of Odin and a phalanx of the dead."

"Which was why you didn't associate the stag with it."

Blake nodded. "Although, when you mentioned it, older tales clicked into place."

I started stacking the books and scrolls. Blake stopped me and sent them back to their respective places with a wave of his hand.

"You do understand why I have to figure this out," I ventured.

"You mean the stag and how it weaves into the future?" Blake arched a dark brow.

I nodded. "Until I can answer that, I have no idea where to focus my energies."

"It might be decided for you. Want to hear about the council gathering?"

I did, but not with the same fervor he expected. "How about dinner first?" I suggested.

"Of course. It should be laid out in our rooms." He draped an arm over my shoulders. Nothing more to do here. All the source documents had returned to their respective shelves.

Together, we walked out of the library. This time, I paid attention to the route, but it could easily change. Magical worlds control who accesses what. There might come a time when my library privileges were revoked. The thought made me smile.

"What?" Blake nudged my side.

"Nothing. Just getting used to things here."

"Excellent. I was afraid the first place you'd go was that office of yours."

His statement stopped me in my tracks. "What if I had gone there?" I tapped a foot as I waited for an answer.

"Then I'd have found you and brought us back here for supper so long as you were willing."

I trained my eyes on the ground and muttered, "Sorry."

"For what?"

"Being prickly. I'll get over it."

He opened his arms. I walked into them. "What if I love you just the way you are?"

Rather than demanding if it were true, no matter what I did or where I went, I wisely kept my mouth shut. We started walking again, and I vowed to focus on dinner and listening to how his time with the council had unfolded.

Marriage was new—for both of us. I'd do well to hold that front and center.

"Abria?"

"Nothing. I love you. What's for dinner?"

As he rattled off dishes, I appreciated food I hadn't had a hand in preparing materializing at will. My new arrangement held plenty of benefits.

And a few drawbacks, a sour inner voice cut in. I shushed it as we walked beneath the lintel and into our rooms.

CHAPTER 4
BLAKE

We ate in companionable silence sitting next to one another. It gave me time to pick and choose which aspects of today's council meeting to highlight. I'd figured Abria would want to know what was said right away, but she'd made it clear she wanted to eat first. I didn't blame her. My often obstreperous minions weren't her problem.

I'd hauled way more baggage into our union than she had.

A big part of that baggage was the Cait Sidhe. They blamed us for losing their home, and they weren't all that far off the mark. Earth hadn't been pleased with their slovenly ways, but my presence spurred her into creating the seismic activity that wiped out their cave system.

Angry, disenfranchised, they had nowhere to go. I finally manned up and shaped a spell to permanently bar them from Underhill. It wasn't as tough as I'd expected, mostly because I was still aghast at the way they'd been living. Eh, *living* put too kind a spin on it. Wallowing in their own filth was closer to the actuality.

My spell meant I'd thrown in the towel on hoping they'd come to their senses and return to the fold one day.

Our sentries had detected them skulking around here since their home was smushed by Earth's relentless disgust. It was only a matter of time before they retaliated. What form it would take remained to be seen. Many of my Cait cousins are gifted magically. If I didn't stay one step ahead of them, they'd defeat my barriers by masquerading as garden-variety Sidhe.

Abria laid a hand on my arm. "Thanks for giving me a bit of space. Still trying to wrap my mind around the Hunt and why it's drawing me into its web."

I was, too. If Odin sat behind this in some twisted way, I wouldn't rest until I had it out with him. Abria was mine. She had no link to the Nine Worlds.

She smiled. "I like the part about being yours."

Oops. I grinned back. "Guess I need to do a better job shielding my thoughts."

"Only if you have something to hide. Do you?" She arched a brow.

"Nay. Not from you."

A burst of power drove me to my feet, hands raised to deal with whoever had the temerity to violate my quarters. A series of hoots told me I'd overreacted.

Hedrek fluttered through a rent in the air and perched on the edge of the table. Four times the size of a normal barn owl, he had tawny feathers and golden eyes. "Abel and

Marika are safely returned from spying on the Cait," he announced.

"What happened?" Abria's tone was sharp. "Are they all right?"

"The Cait haven't thought clearly since their caves blew up. I've been keeping an eye on the cats, and it didn't feel safe to leave them spying on the Cait a moment longer."

"Good thing one of us was on top of this," Abria said tartly and set her mouth in a tight line. "I should have been the one watching over them. I'm who asked them to help. They were my responsibility, and—"

Hedrek pecked her hand. "Consider it my wedding gift. The two of you deserved some time alone together."

"Where are they?" I asked the owl.

"Outside your door. They hate journey spells, so I spared them the last part of this one."

Abria was on her feet in a trice running for the door. She flung it open and bent to gather the two alley cats into her arms cooing and telling them how wonderful and brave they'd been.

Abel, a large black tomcat with part of one ear missing and green eyes wriggled out of her grip, meowing fiercely. Marika, a calico, draped herself around Abria's neck.

"I still say we could have remained." Abel jumped on the table and stuck his snout into a fish dish smothered in delicate cream sauce.

Abria set Marika on the table next to Abel. "Help yourselves"—she made shooing motions—"we were done, anyway."

"Do you know anything?" I asked the owl.

"There were many disagreements, a lot of infighting. Zottre, their leader, became unpredictable. After he banished two of his own for supposed treason, I extricated Abel and Marika."

Abel had moved on to the remains of a quiche. He looked up long enough to say, "The two who were banished did nothing wrong. Zottre has turned into a maniac. Labritha gathered followers of her own and is planning to take over—if she can."

Hedrek clacked his beak. "Solid reasons to whisk you to safety."

Abel sat on his haunches and proceeded to lick his paws and clean his whiskers. "I disagree. You should have left us there long enough to see if Labritha was successful. She's more cutthroat than Zottre."

"My assessment as well," I murmured. "How many allies have committed to her?"

"Around half the Cait," Marika replied. "Makes it difficult to predict who will prevail."

I'd put my money on Labritha any day. She'd never had any scruples, and fighting dirty was the only way she knew.

"If you're done eating"—Abria addressed the cats— "would you like me to return you to Nairn. I'm certain the rest of your kin are worried about you."

"You should return us to the Cait," Abel insisted.

"They probably haven't missed us yet," Marika added. "Too busy fighting among themselves."

"Is there any chance your magic was detected?" I asked Hedrek.

Feathers rustled. "There's always a chance, but no one came after us."

I exchanged glances with Abria. "What do you think?"

"It's too risky," she answered. "Bits of residual magic are bound to cling to them. It could be because I'm attuned to it, but I feel Hedrek's energy."

"That's because I'm right next to you," the owl said tartly.

Abria turned to him. "I sense it on the cats too. It's faint, and someone would have to be looking for it, but if anyone went hunting for Abel or Marika and didn't find them..."

I got the drift. If the cats had been part of the landscape before, them being gone for a while could move them to a place with more intense scrutiny. After getting to my feet, I bowed formally. "I extend thanks on behalf of the Sidhe. Know that we are in your debt and will return your sacrifice as we can."

A low growl issued from Abel. "Fancy way of telling us we're done."

"It isn't like that—" Abria began.

"Then what is it like?" Marika swiped a pink tongue over her lips.

"I have to leave for a while," Abria explained. "Hedrek may come with me. Blake won't have time to keep an eye on you."

"No one has 'kept an eye on me' since I was a kitten," Abel said sourly.

Abria scooped him into her arms. "Dear-heart. I want you to live long enough to fight more battles and father more kittens. A while back, a wolf died during a wraith attack in Inverness. I was the target, and I still haven't forgiven myself for his death." She exhaled sharply. "I refuse to allow your loyalty and devotion to me to spell your demise."

"It shouldn't be your choice," Marika said stoutly, "but ours."

Abria shook her head. "Your usual self-preservation instincts are clouded by your links with me. What kind of person would I be to take advantage of you like that?"

Abel wriggled in her arms; she put him down.

I glanced from the cats to Hedrek to Abria. We'd clearly reached an impasse. "Return to your kinfolk," I told the cats. "Once there, gather everyone and see who would be willing to join us in battle."

"How do you know it will come to that?" Abel asked.

"The Cait were undecided as to what to do next," Marika chimed in. "Many counseled a full-on war, but many others labeled it a fool's errand."

"We can do more good on the inside," Abel insisted.

An idea rattled around in my mind. "I can instill temporary magic in the two of you. If you're sparing how you use it—"

"No!" Abria slammed the flat of her hand on the tabletop making the dishes rattle. "It's far too dangerous. The Cait may be deranged, but they'll sense any alteration in Abel and Marika. It's a sure bet they've been examined up one side and down the other."

"If I'm going to return them," Hedrek spoke up, "it must be soon."

"We want to go back." Abel meowed loudly to punctuate

his words. Cat speech is quite garbled, but if you listen to enough of it, it's understandable.

Abria turned her hands palms up. "Okay. I give up, but I will return you."

"It's not far from here," Hedrek informed us and followed his words with a series of images.

"I know the spot," Abria said and turned to the cats. "I will take us there. If I do not deem it safe, I'll return you to Nairn."

"How are you going to determine safety?" I asked.

"Simple. I'll be there, skulking on the sidelines, until I'm satisfied no harm will come to them."

I didn't like the sound of that. "Do not engage them, Abria."

She rounded on me. "You may be my mate, but it does not give you the right to tell me what to do."

"Remember Rait Castle? Roya jumped in to save you."

Abria flapped a hand at me. "That was before I learned to augment my ability. And before Underhill recognized me as a friend." Her tone softened. "You married me for chrissakes. Now is not the time to discover you don't trust my judgement."

She'd caught me dead to rights. My cheeks warmed with something between shame and guilt. "It's not that I don't trust you."

"Oh?" She placed her hands on her hips. "Then what is it?"

"I was spawned by a different era, one where men took care of women."

Abria shook her head. "Not going to work, Sir Galahad. I

came from the same era and found it stifling and ridiculous. We can hash this out later. Every second that passes makes this riskier."

After motioning to the cats, who scurried to her, she constructed a hasty spell and left.

I summoned magic of my own.

"What do you think you're doing?" Hedrek inquired.

"Going after her. What else?"

He flew in front of me, wings spread. "Bad idea, mate. She's already convinced you don't have faith in her."

I dropped my hands to my sides. Much as I hated to admit it, the owl was right. "What am I supposed to do?" I growled. "Pace from one end of my rooms to the other and stew until she returns? If I conjure a spell to keep an eye on her, she'll feel it."

"Spying isn't the right approach, either. I'm certain the Sidhe prince can find a better use for his time."

"Do not mock me." Annoyed, I inserted spaces between each word.

He clacked his beak. "Take it as you will."

My earlier time with Abria came roaring to the forefront. Before I could debate the wisdom of my question, I blurted, "Did you ever ride with Odin and his Hunt?"

If an owl can look surprised, Hedrek did. His eyes grew more rounded; his beak hung open. His expression gave me all the answer I needed.

"Next question is why you quit?" I said.

"How did you find out?"

"It's in a few of the older lore books."

The owl's wings were already spread; he took to the air

and flew circles around the room. "Those records were to be expunged," he hooted.

I shrugged. "Maybe most of them were. Our Sidhe library predates my existence by a thousand years. And it isn't accessible to just anyone, so whoever was responsible for blotting out that bit of history probably missed us."

Hedrek continued to scribe circles around my great room. So far, he hadn't been particularly forthcoming with answers, but I wasn't done.

"Any idea why Odin wants Abria?"

"How do you know he does?" the owl countered and lit on the edge of a table. He'd leave scratches in the wood from his talons, but it was the least of my concerns.

"Because Abria has been dreaming about the Hunt."

"I knew but lacked details."

Nodding, I added, "She's riding at the head of a large company of warriors on Becca with an enormous golden stag by her side."

Hoots filled the air. So many the owl had to be upset. "You must know the stag," I pressed. "He was in the eldritch lore books along with you."

I'd done as much as I could. Now it was a matter of waiting for Hedrek to decide if I was worth confiding in. I ferried dishes into the kitchen and set a minor household spell to take care of them. When I returned, snifter of brandy in hand, the owl had perched on the arm of my favorite easy chair and was shredding the fabric.

"Figured you'd return," he muttered.

I nodded pleasantly. "Just as I figured you'd remain. We

both care about Abria. Any information you hold is more than I have currently."

The owl fluffed his feathers until he appeared even larger than normal. "Odin was a different regent when he first created the Wild Hunt."

"Different, how?"

"Softer, more compassionate. Involved with the animal world. He left Hel to tend to the dead, and the giants hadn't yet taken over Jotunheim. Yggdrasil was young, carefree. Everyone was welcome in the Norse realm."

News to me. This was a version of Odin and his kingdom I'd never suspected existed.

"You may know some of this," Hedrek continued. "The stag is actually Herne, god of forests and game animals. He wears horns from a great stag and has done so for so long he appears to be one. He's considered divine and was the first leader of the Hunt with a great horn, a wooden bow, and a mighty black steed. Eventually, he merged with the stag and no longer rode the horse."

"Go on." I crooked two fingers at the owl.

He fluffed his feathers. "Not much more to tell. Mortals who got in the way of Herne's hunt were swept up in it, destined to ride with him for all eternity. Odin was eaten up with jealousy. From his way of looking at things, the dead belonged to him."

"Let me guess," I broke in. "They had it out, and Odin won."

Hedrek hooted mournfully. "When Odin took over, all of us who rode with the Hunt left. He rebuilt it to his liking."

"What happened to Herne?"

"No one knows, but it was rumored he died from a broken heart. The Hunt was a lynchpin of his existence."

I blew out a breath. "Maybe he didn't die."

"What do you mean?" The owl moved from the arm of my chair and lit in front of where I stood.

"Abria could be dreaming of him because he's planning to wrest the Hunt back from Odin. Somehow he discovered the extent of her power and wants her as an ally."

"You have no way of knowing," the owl said firmly.

"Not right now, but I'll see if I can't find him." One thing was certain. Herne wasn't going to shanghai Abria. Not on my watch, or ever. We did not need Odin as a sworn enemy.

"Best of luck," the owl hooted.

"What's that supposed to mean?"

"No one's seen Herne in over a thousand years."

"If you're trying to dissuade me, you'll have to do better than that." On a whim, I asked, "Want to come along?"

The pause that stretched between us was so long, I felt certain he'd say no. Meanwhile, I walked into the bedchamber and changed into clothes more suitable for traipsing around the muddy countryside—or time traveling. If I couldn't locate Herne in the present, I'd search the past.

"Aye," came from the sitting room. "I will accompany you. I'd like to see Herne again."

"Any idea where to begin our search?" I called.

"Some. Are you ready?"

Building a travel spell as I walked, I joined him. "Never readier."

CHAPTER 5
ABRIA

Hedrek had highlighted a spot just under Ben Kilbreck, southwest of Loch Rimsdale, deep in the northern Highlands. Once said to be a stronghold for the Tuatha de Dannan, the peak was rumored to house Leprechauns and Brownies beneath its bulk.

The cats mewled and squirmed in my arms.

"Quiet. We're nearly there."

In case the Cait had posted sentries, I deepened my warding. No one would be expecting me, which helped. The far northern reaches of Scotland are devoid of trees, but there are plenty of boulders. I brought us out in a circle of standing stones. Many had tumbled onto their sides.

My feet squelched in the ever-present mud. Humidity pressed on me like a winding sheet. Scotland was gorgeous and green, but the farther north you went, the colder and wetter it became.

Abel and Marika wiggled harder. Clearly, they wanted me to put them down.

"Not yet," I cautioned and sent a weak beam of power arcing in a full circle to assess who else was here beyond the odd mortal traipsing this way and that. With fancy cameras slung around their necks and overly loud voices, most of them were probably American tourists.

If there were sentries, I couldn't locate them.

"Where's the entry point?" I asked the cats.

Images flooded my mind, and I glided to the far side of an enormous boulder, intent on getting as close to the entrance as possible. Before I'd rounded the bulk of the peak, several puffs of magic flowed between me and my destination.

Not the Cait.

Not a Celt.

Narrowing my focus, I sorted through various possibilities and came up with goose eggs.

I sank into a crouch and set the cats on the muddy ground. *"Stay put."*

"But—" Abel began.

"No buts." I added compulsion to my stay put command. Normally, I'd never have held any animal against its will, but I couldn't split my attention. Whatever was heading our way was almost here.

The puffs of magic turned into Leprechauns. Hundreds of them. They're on the smallish side, maybe a meter to a meter-and-a-half tall with pointy chins and ears. Contrary to urban myth, they aren't green. A male with long golden hair and brown eyes sidled close and touched my arm with tentative fingers.

"Och, and ye're real," he breathed.

"Can you hear mind speech?" At his nod, I went on. *"So far, no one but you knows we're here. I'd like to keep it that way."*

The same enchantment that had cloaked them clicked back into place. Suddenly, the only one I could see was the man who'd spoken. *"Thank you."* I inclined my head.

"Will you help us?" Before I could inquire what he needed, he hurried on, *"We prayed for Danu to come, but she hasn't. And then you arrived. Did she send you?"*

"No. Sorry."

The Leprechaun looked so crestfallen, I felt for his plight. *"What's the matter? Why do you require divine intervention?"*

"Sidhe have taken over our home." He punched the air with a tiny fist. *"'Tis been ours since the beginnings of time. They have no right."*

Abel nudged me. *"We're going to sneak inside."*

"Not without me, you're not." I touched the Leprechaun's shoulder. *"Wait here. I shall return."* I'd correct their impression that every Sidhe was behind the loss of their home later.

I made a grab for Abel, but he and Marika sprinted ahead. It was all I could do to keep a ward over them. Once we rounded the corner of Ben Kilbreck, I spied two holes drilled into the side of the mountain. They were patched over with magic. Mortals wouldn't have noticed them, but to me they were clear as day.

Marika's tail was just vanishing into the lefthand one. Presumably, Abel had entered before her. I adjusted my warding to make it less noticeable—hopefully—and followed them inside.

The same rank odor that had permeated their last home on a South Pacific Island hit me like a wall. More than anything, it screamed the Cait Sidhe had lost their minds and their dignity. No wonder Blake was disgusted with them and brokenhearted too. They were still Sidhe, no matter how far they'd fallen, and he was bound to protect all his kinsmen.

Gloom accompanied the stench, but enough light filtered in from the two entry points to see unaided. Abel and Marika huddled in a hollowed-out spot about ten meters ahead. I remained midway between them and where we'd come into the underground lair. Close enough to keep control of the warding protecting them.

Water dripped down the walls. It smelled of salt and metal. Fist-sized crystals studded the walls in a rainbow of colors. Scottish peaks are some of the oldest on Earth. Formed by uplifting, they carried remnants of the sea and Neptune's crafty hand.

Powerful magic surrounded me: Celtic enchantment so thick you could cut it with a knife. How had the Cait worked around it? Even at my skill level, every instinct I had shouted to leave immediately. I wasn't welcome here. Bad things would happen if I remained.

Empty threats, but they'd served the Celts well and preserved this sacred space for their pets. Unhappy pets waiting for me to return and save them.

I settled in to wait and loosened the edges of my ward to allow the cats to creep out whenever they deemed it safe.

They'd feel the alteration in the weave of my spell. Even animals that don't carry power of their own are exquisitely sensitive to it.

The occasional Cait sauntered past. When a pair looking this way and that, obviously hunting for something, passed by, Abel waited until they were a hundred paces ahead before he and Marika glided into the center of the passageway.

Hissing and spitting, they tussled with one another until fur flew this way and that. The Cait who'd just walked past hurried back.

"Where have the two of you been?" one demanded.

Abel and Marika kept right on batting at one another as they rolled on the dusty floor.

"We're talking with you," the other Cait shouted and clipped Abel with the toe of his boot.

The black tomcat jumped straight up into the air, whirled, and landed on all fours spitting and yowling at the Cait. Marika joined him, standing shoulder-to-shoulder. I added the unmistakable scent of feline heat to her hind end. She caught a whiff and bumped her butt into Abel.

A possessive meow from him meant he'd gladly play along. What male wouldn't?

Apparently, the cats hadn't let on they could respond to any form of speech. Smart of them. One Cait elbowed the other, his mouth spread in a knowing leer. "Mystery solved," he announced.

"Maybe we'll get in on the action." The other grinned nastily. His cock rose, curving against his belly, and he stroked it with practiced fingers.

For the most part, the Cait don't bother with clothes. Shapeshifting is far easier when you don't have to stop to disrobe first. The one with the obvious hard-on developed a translucent aspect, well on his way to adopting his feline form.

Abel growled low and menacing. Hackles rose the length of his spine, and he reared back, claws extended.

"Not worth it, Brin." The first Cait chopped a hand in front of his companion, effectively stopping his shift.

"Of course, it is," the other Cait sputtered. "She's gorgeous."

Abel growled louder and swiped his claws down Brin's shin.

"Ouch!" The Cait jumped back. "You little bastard. I could fry you with a thought."

Oh-oh. I readied power as surreptitiously as I could, but I wasn't as sly as I'd hoped. Two sets of eyes snapped in my direction searching for the source of the disturbance.

Abel and Marika took off at a dead run.

They were safe. Now all I had to do was get myself out of here. Withdrawing every scrap of my essence behind bombproof warding, I kept still and waited. The Cait came within centimeters of my position, but I didn't dare move. If it weren't for Abel and Marika, I'd flatten them both and have done with it, but the proximity to the cats' presence was suspicious. It just might push the Cait to take a deeper look at their disappearance. I couldn't risk their safety, so I put up with the reek as it filled my nostrils and made my gorge rise in protest.

"I tell you I felt something," Brin muttered.

"Yeah, your dick turned what passes for brains to mush," the other Cait snarled.

"You're jealous yours isn't bigger."

"Is that right?" Brin's buddy flipped around and punched him in the guts.

Go for it. I silently cheered them on.

When Brin lit into the other Cait, I wound my ward tight around me and hustled for an exit point. Consumed by trying to inflict maximum damage, neither paid me the slightest heed.

Daylight surrounded me. Rain joined it, pelting my body with large, lazy drops. The Scots should have more than one word for rain. It has as many variations as the setting sun. I hurried back to where I'd left the Leprechaun horde and puzzled over the Cait.

Something had happened to distort their loyalties. From the looks of things, they weren't even devoted to one another. They'd forged an uneasy alliance with Satan. Had the king of Hell twisted something in their makeup? Perverted it to his benefit?

Seemed likely, but I'd kick it around with Blake.

Hedrek would have to return to his post watching out for Abel and Marika. The more I saw of the Cait, the less I trusted them. Having an enemy is one thing, but enemies who no longer ascribe to rational thought is something else altogether.

The Leprechauns huddled in the rain like a flock of drenched geese. Rain ran off their heads, pooling around sodden garments.

"You came back." The one who'd spoken with me before sounded surprised.

"Took you long enough," another man muttered.

I started to explain Abel and Marika were my responsibility but didn't. The cats meant nothing to this bunch. *"Of course, I came back, but I'm not sure there's much I can do to help."*

Dejected expressions, heavy with accusation, met my gaze. Leprechauns held the luck and fortunes of the world. Who wouldn't want to help them? A bigger question was why Danu hadn't stepped in. Ben Kilbreck was her purview.

"It's not all the Sidhe who've taken over your home," I explained. *"Only the Cait Sidhe. They broke from the others a long while back."*

"Can't whoever heads up the rest of them do something?" The one who seemed to be the group spokesman asked.

"He's trying." I was tempted to make excuses for Blake but didn't. Nothing I could say would erase the ignominy of being booted from their home.

"Does he know about us?" the Leprechaun pressed.

"I'll make certain he does." I aimed for a reassuring tone and then added, *"I have no way of contacting Danu, but I will ensure Arianrhod knows about this."*

"What good is she?" someone muttered.

"Presumably, she knows Danu," I replied.

"What are we supposed to do in the meantime?" another Leprechaun asked.

Sheesh. It was like dealing with a group of entitled children. But then I reminded myself one of the gods had always taken care of them. It wasn't the type of arrangement suited to development of independent thinking.

"What have you been doing?" I was genuinely curious.

The male I'd been speaking with said, *"Keeping everyone together, but 'tisn't easy."*

I frowned. *"Why not. Where would you go if not here?"*

"Our assigned portion of the Highlands," a slender female answered. Violet hair was braided tight against her head; rain spilled down her shoulders, and her sodden skirts clung to her legs. She was barefoot like all the rest of her kin.

Hmmm. This was getting murkier and murkier. I'd had no idea the little people had assigned anythings. *"What do you do in these designated spots?"* I glanced around the group.

"Mortals leave offerings." The leader cocked his head to one side. *"Do you not know anything about us?"*

"Very little." I confirmed his suspicions. *"I need to scurry back to Underhill, but I'll discuss your problem with Blake."*

"Who's he?"

"Elwyn Cardassier."

A collective sigh ran through the group. Clearly, they knew Blake by his eldritch name. *"Like that's going to do a scrap of good,"* someone mumbled.

"Meanwhile," I went on, *"do you need anything else right now?"*

"Besides our home returned to us?" The violet-haired woman's question dripped derision.

I wasn't doing much good here. They were starting to view me as useless, a far cry from the savior they'd hoped I would be.

A familiar hoot broke into my mental funk. Hedrek

winged closer, flew a couple of broad circles, and landed next to me.

"*What happened?*" the owl squawked.

"*Abel and Marika are safe, but the Cait displaced all these good folk*"—I spread my arms wide—"*from their home.*"

Hedrek focused on the Leprechauns. "*Where is Danu?*" he demanded. "*She is your protector.*"

The one I assumed was their leader faced the owl. They were about the same height, but the owl much broader. "*We have not seen her for many a long year,*" the Leprechaun admitted."

"*Can you ask Arianrhod to chase her down?*" I arched a brow the owl's way.

He shrugged along with rustling feathers. "*I can try.*"

Talk about cryptic. My take was Arianrhod hadn't seen Danu for a long time, either, but I kept the interpretation to myself.

"*After you do that,*" I went on, "*could you continue to keep an eye on the cats?*" I stopped there. No reason to go into all the gritty details about how Abel and Marika had inveigled their way back inside.

"*Certainly.*" The owl broke into motes of golden light and disappeared.

I turned my attention to the Leprechauns. All of us were soaked clear through. "*Is there somewhere you can get out of the weather?*" Seeing nods, I made shooing motions with both hands. "*Get moving. Someone will return with news.*"

"*By when?*" The leader was trying, but despondency wove through his question.

"*Not all that long. A few days at the most.*"

He bobbed his head my way. The group turned as a unit and walked briskly across the meadow, vanishing into Highland mist.

I doubled up a fist and punched it into my palm. Damn the Cait Sidhe. I should have done far more than end their leader that night at Rait Castle. I should have wiped out the whole bloody mess.

Not that I'd been in any kind of shape to do shit once they chucked me deep into Underhill, a place that doesn't exactly welcome strangers. I turned in a full circle, surveying the drenched moorlands. My people—the rodents, birds, and insects—were nowhere to be found. Wise of them. No one wandered about in the midst of Scotland's frequent deluges.

I was thoroughly soaked too, but it was the least of my worries. Everywhere the Cait landed created discontent. The Earth goddess had wielded the upper hand, ousting them from their last home. This time, they'd taken care to select an adversary who couldn't fight back.

I wiped rain out of my eyes and shook my head. Wet hair swung this way and that. Why couldn't Earth intervene here as well? Surely, she commanded these lands. Why wasn't she as outraged to have her realm sullied here? Or did it take her time to react?

The more I thought about it, the more likely the latter interpretation was to be true. She was spirit, not corporeal in any sense of the word. Not much more for me to do here. I considered waiting for Hedrek to return, decided it was a sound idea, and trotted back across the muddy meadow. Once he'd reported in, then I'd return to Underhill.

When I drew close to the hole I'd originally entered, the sound of raised voices beat against my ears even over the howl of the wind.

Eavesdropping can be most instructive. After dropping a ward over myself, I crept closer intent on finding out everything I could. Spying was Abel and Marika's job, but so long as I was here, I'd collect intel from my end too. The cats would have the context I lacked.

"Never any such thing as too much information," I muttered half to myself and settled in to listen.

CHAPTER 6
BLAKE

Locating Herne proved far more difficult than I'd imagined. After checking all of the Nine Worlds, a few border worlds, and what I thought might be likely spots on Earth, I wasn't any closer to finding him. Neither had anyone I spoke with seen or talked with him in at least two centuries.

Hedrek dropped out of the search shortly after we left the Nine Worlds. He might want to lay eyes on Herne again, but he was more concerned about Abria and the cats.

I didn't exactly comb through Odin's demesne. More of a cursory search since I didn't want to deal with Hel or the frost giants or the band of dead warriors. I've never figured out if the current complement for the Wild Hunt lives in Niflheim—with Hel guarding them—or if they got promoted to Valhalla for however long their tenure in the Hunt lasted.

None of it mattered. What did was that my search to

date was far from promising.

Maybe my theory about Herne trying to coopt Abria had been way off the mark. He could be well and truly dead since he carried mortal blood along with divine essence. But if he was dead, what had happened to the magical stag?

I wasn't too far from Windsor Castle; I'd been trying to figure out which oak was Herne's. Legends suggested the original tree had been chopped down in the 1600s, and that replanted ones had met with a similar fate.

A lad speeding by on a bicycle almost clipped me from behind. I started to shout at him to pay closer attention, but was loathe to draw attention to myself. He swerved past, blond locks flying in a brisk breeze.

Moving out of the flow of humanity and traffic, I settled on a bench and dredged what I knew about Herne from rusty memory banks. He was supposed to show up on the brink of natural disasters and the deaths of kings. Not much help there. England hadn't had a king in a very long time. Not since George VI died in 1952. I wasn't certain what constituted a natural disaster. Most current ones were manmade.

Breath steamed from between my teeth making clouds in the chilly air. Past time to return to Underhill since I wasn't making any progress here.

This wasn't a good spot to disappear from. Too many passersby.

I lumbered to my feet, feeling discouraged. I'd been confident in my mission when I'd begun. Not any longer. Should I take another spin past the Nine Worlds? I'd been stealthy, barely skimming the surface in my concern not to disturb anyone. Odin's temper was legendary. I had no good reason for breaching his borders, and he'd sniff out a lie from a mile away.

It took a good quarter hour to find a private enough spot to launch a journey spell. Gods, the UK has grown unbelievably crowded. How had I not noticed? Crouched in a fetid ally between two fifteenth century buildings, I considered my options again.

My search for Herne had turned up one dead end after another. I'd discarded the idea of time traveling. Even if I found a long-ago version of Herne, he'd have no idea how his future would unfold.

Locating Odin would prove far simpler, but what could I tell him? And did I really want to run the gauntlet of his fury when I presented myself at Valhalla's golden gates? He's never needed a reason to be pissed off. A foul mood is where he lives. I could be mistaken about the lack of a warm reception, but he wasn't the back-slapping, bonhomie type.

I sought a winning combination of explanations for my sudden appearance and abandoned each one as soon as it tripped across my mind.

Try the truth, mate, an inner voice suggested dryly.

Not going to fly, I answered.

If I threw myself on Odin's mercy—he didn't have any— and told him my mate had been dreaming of the Hunt, he'd assume it was a sign for his motley crop of dead warriors to pass her amongst them.

Not that Abria would stand for it.

Regardless, I did not want to draw the Norse god's awareness her way.

Drunken voices grew louder. Judging from ribald commentary, a loose woman and her latest mark had decided the alley was quicker and cheaper than renting a room.

No more time to dither this way and that.

I'd already constructed a spell. Loosing it, I departed quickly. Startled gasps suggested I'd left a light trail, but the couple would chalk it up to being drunk.

I hoped.

Casting magic within eye- or earshot of mortals is forbidden. Not that anyone would turn me in. I chuckled. Nowhere to turn me in to. Since the Celts had decamped, I was the highest agent left.

Odin wouldn't agree. In his mind, his authority trumped all else, but he was wrong about that. The only place he held dominion was eight of the Nine Worlds.

I narrowed my eyes. I'd been so fixated on Odin and his ilk, I hadn't considered others who might have news of the horned god. Arianrhod had her finger on the pulse of everything magical. Cailleach as well.

I couldn't switch gears in the middle of a journey spell, but the moment I touched down in a remote corner of Asgard, I'd switch things up and leave for Caer Sidi. If luck was with me, Arianrhod hadn't moved it since Abria and I left.

Power hummed along my nerve endings. The golden vista of Asgard glistened and shimmied but refused to totally wink out. Damn it. Had I been discovered? Or were the frequencies here incompatible with my skills?

It had never been the case before, but someone could

have discovered my previous visit and instituted a counter-spell to snare me should I be stupid enough to return.

I added velocity to my casting. It doubled back and smacked me across my third eye. Pain shot through my head; a nail gun driving spikes through my forehead wouldn't have hurt more. Asgard quit whirling, a sure sign my spell had failed.

"They told me it was you. I didn't believe you'd be this arrogant. Or this stupid." Odin's deep, gravelly voice spun me around. He always looks the same. A mountain of a god, he stands slightly more than two meters. Almost as broad as he is tall, his naked neck, back and shoulders were slabbed with muscle. A scraggly silver beard reached to mid-chest. Leather breeks covered him from waist to ankle, clinging like a second skin. His battle axe was strapped across his back with stout leather thongs. Large, black ravens, Huginn and Muninn, graced both shoulders.

His single gray eye was fixed on me. I stood tall beneath his scrutiny and reminded myself he wasn't any better than me. Worse, in fact, since he totally lacked compassion.

"Aye. It's me," I agreed jauntily.

He took a swing at me with a meaty fist. I ducked out of its path. One of the ravens squawked, presumably requesting leave to peck out my eyes. Odin barked something in return, and the bird stayed put.

"Why. Are. You. Here. Twice?" He inserted spaces between the words to ensure I was able to follow them. His assumption I was operating with less than a full deck pissed me off, but reacting would reduce me to his level.

Rather than answering directly, I offered an engaging

smile. "How's the Hunt been of late?"

His thick features developed furrows as he tried to determine what I was up to. "What's it to you?" he growled.

"Just wondering." I was fishing but added, "Saw all of you in the skies the other night, and—"

"That's a goddess-damned lie," he thundered and took another swipe at me. Because he's so clunky, evading him was simple. Once he loosed the ravens—or summoned a dragon or two—any advantage I had would fritter to nothing.

Interesting. Meant the Hunt wasn't active for some reason.

"You have two minutes," Odin went on, "to explain yourself."

I planted my feet shoulder width, arms swinging by my sides and asked, "What happens then?"

"I happen then." Hel shimmered into corporeality by Odin's side. I've only seen her a few times, and the sight is damned disconcerting. Half her body is bones, the other part covered with skin. Nearly as tall as Odin, but lithe and long limbed, she had black hair that fell to waist level on the flesh side. Dark eyes regarded me with interest, as if I were a choice morsel to play with. A richly embroidered green silk robe hung open in the front, displaying one lush breast and a rack of ribs.

Her two serpents, hooded black cobras, hissed at me.

I looked from her to Odin. Hel was Loki's daughter. Loki and Odin were blood brothers, so, in some unnatural fashion, he was sort of an uncle to her. Still, he'd found her appearance so distasteful, he banished her to Niflheim.

Odin shrugged. "Time's up, Sidhe."

"Ooooh, means he's mine," Hel purred.

Her serpents glided my way. Choices were being made for me, but it didn't mean I had to lie down and play dead. I raised a hand; power arced from my fingertips. One of the serpents hissed and swayed but stopped in his tracks.

"What have you done to him?" Hel screeched and threw her body over her pet.

"Nothing yet," I replied, followed by, "Is this how you usually treat mages who visit your realm?"

Hel still huddled over her snake cooing in Old Norse. The other cobra wound protective coils around them both. Blood dripped down an exposed cheekbone, lending Hel an even more macabre appearance.

"You were not invited," Odin growled in response to my question.

My turn to shrug. "Maybe not. No way to reach you other than dropping in." I spoke true, and he knew as much.

He bared yellowed teeth. "I've extended you grace past my two-minute warning, but if you do not tell me why you've breached my borders immediately, I'll let Hel have you." His lips formed a knowing leer. "She's fancied you for a long while."

Hel? News to me. I glanced sidelong at her, but she was focused on her injured serpent.

"The reason I'm here is simple," I replied. "I'm looking for Herne. Have you seen him?"

"You're looking for him here? Why?" Odin shot back.

The ravens squawked in outrage. Odin dragged his axe from its sheath and chucked it into a nearby tree. The tree shook its boughs and made a hissing noise not unlike the snakes. It creaked and heaved until the axe popped free, falling to the ground.

Goddess's tits, was everything in this realm sentient?

"Why are you hunting Herne here?" Odin repeated.

"Because he isn't anywhere else." I didn't add anything about his association with the Hunt. Odin only appeared dimwitted. He'd connect the dots soon enough if he hadn't already.

"What do you want with him?" Hel screwed her features into a disgusted moue.

I trod carefully. "Some of my subjects have been dreaming about him."

"Since when do you care enough about them to chase anything down?" Odin sneered.

I bit back a tart reply. If anyone didn't give a crap about his people, it was Odin. Granted I hadn't been overly present for a few centuries, but that was the old me.

Hel straightened, staring me down. "Tell me about these dreams, Sidhe."

Too late, I remembered she was a seer, but then, so was Odin. It was why he'd hung from Yggdrasil for nine days and nights long ago: to curry the accompanying visions.

Proceeding carefully, threading truth with fiction, I replied, "When my subjects dream of Herne, I want to know why."

Odin's one eye widened. Before he could say anything, Hel stepped between us. "What do they see in these dreams?"

An obvious truth net clanked over my head, covering me

to the dirt I stood upon. Fine. So much for floating lies, but it didn't compel me to speak. We stood like some unholy frozen tableau until Odin snapped, "Release him."

"But he hasn't said anything," Hel protested.

"Nor will he," Odin muttered.

Like I said, Odin only appears dumber than a box of rocks. Waiting for me to reveal anything would plunk us here until Midgard was absorbed back into Earth's solar system.

Odin crooked a finger my way. "Follow me, Sidhe."

Oh-oh. "Where are we going?"

"You'll find out when we get there. Are you coming or no?"

"What about him coming with me?" Hel shrilled.

Odin eyed me. "Do you wish to accompany Hel?"

I floundered about hunting for a graceful way out. Bowing low in her direction, I said, "I appreciate the offer, but I'm recently mated."

She looked askance at me. "What difference does that make?"

"Coming?" Odin snatched up his axe, sheathed it, and lumbered off. He'd had enough of Hel's questions and clearly could give a fuck less where I went. It probably meant I'd be free to teleport out of here, but I was curious.

If he meant me harm, he'd have challenged me to a duel, or called in the dragons, or the giants. After waving a cheery goodbye to Hel, I loped after Odin. He moved quicker than his bulk suggested was possible.

We walked in silence through Asgard's golden streets, and up a hill. Valhalla sat on its top. Power zapped me as we crossed a drawbridge over a moat filled with dragonesque heads. Every dragon I've even known has liked its space, but not this bunch.

Another zap as I entered the castle proper. Despite the golden streets and gates, Valhalla was a no-frills operation. Hounds bounded to Odin's side as we traipsed along rough-hewn wooden floors to a large dining hall. A battered trestle table ran the length of the room. Steaming trenchers sat on another table running along the back wall.

Odin motioned to the food. "Help yourself."

Suddenly suspicious, I asked, "Aren't you going to eat?"

Booming laughter burst from him. "If I wanted you dead, Sidhe, there are cleaner ways than poison."

When I filled a plate and returned to the table, Odin pointed to a spot not far from where he'd taken up residence at the table's head. He slopped what smelled like a very young wine into a silver tankard. It floated my way and *thunked* down in front of me.

He drained his tankard, refilled it, and leveled his gaze at me. "Why are you really here?"

"Already told you," I said around a mouthful of a very bland stew. Either Odin wasn't picky, or his preference was hearty fare that had all the panache of cardboard.

"Herne has never even visited the Nine Worlds. Searching for him here makes no sense."

"Apologies. I made a mistake."

He leaned back in his chair and plopped his booted feet on the table. "You chose a mate. Why settle for one when you could have your pick of many?"

"I fell in love. Why else?"

"After thousands of years? With whom?"

I waved a dismissive hand. "You wouldn't know her."

"Try me."

Prickling around the edges of my head alerted me he was going after information the old-fashioned way. I warded my mind and buried anything related to Abria deep.

He slapped a hand on the table. "Don't tell me you married a mortal. How's that going to work? She'll die, and—"

"I did not marry a mortal," I protested.

"Ha. Narrows the field considerably. It can't be a Sidhe. You've known them as long as you've been alive. Can't be a Celt. They're gone. Let's see"—by now, Odin was muttering to himself—"Fae, druid, witch, sorceress."

He snapped his fingers. "Got it. You trolled through the *Dreaming*."

"Why is knowing so important?" I cut into his monologue.

"Why else? Knowledge is power."

The rattling of chains drew my attention from my mediocre meal. Spirits oozed into the dining room. Most were still clad in whatever they'd worn when they died in battle. Hoofs clattered up stairs, and Sleipnir, Odin's eight-legged horse, pranced into the room.

"Damn. Lost track of the time," Odin boomed. His feet thumped to the floor. He sprang onto Sleipnir's broad back. "Remain if you'd like, Sidhe. We can continue our dialogue come morning."

The ravens flew to huge windows at the far end of the chamber. Working as a team, they jockeyed them open with sharp beaks and pulled them aside. Sleipnir sprang through with the dead warriors behind him. The room had filled with the stench of decaying flesh as more and more of the Hunt assembled.

Between the lackluster food and the reek of the dead, any appetite I'd had fled. Alone in the hall, I got my feet under me and walked to the still-open window.

The Hunt may not have graced the skies for a while, but they were on the prowl tonight. Ghost horses joined them, and the smells of leather and hay mingled with rotting flesh.

Was I free to leave?

I'd find out quick enough. The spell that had come back to bite me earlier bloomed once more. This time, it carried me smoothly out of Valhalla to the in-between place. All I had to do was wait out the transit.

Had I misjudged Odin? He'd seemed more intrigued by gossip than warfare, but it could have been an act to get me to drop my guard. I still didn't trust him.

The familiar smells of Underhill rose up to greet me. Wishing I had more to show for my efforts than a hatful of questions, I reeled in my journey casting. It had dumped me out in one of Underhill's many passageways not too far from my chamber.

"There you are." Abria ran toward me. "Don't get too comfortable. The Cait displaced the Leprechauns. You have to do something."

"So? What happened to Danu?" I stopped before whining about why I had to be the one responsible for everything. It wasn't becoming for a Sidhe prince—or for anyone when you got down to it.

"They called her. She never showed up. Hedrek went to talk with Arianrhod, but I haven't heard back from him yet. I waited far longer than I'd planned before finally returning here. Means Abel and Marika have no one standing guard over them."

She hooked a hand through my arm and crinkled her nose. "You smell nasty. Where have you been?"

"Long story. I'll clean up."

"No time for that. We have to get moving. I promised the Leprechauns."

"Huh? Promised them what? And what were you doing near Ben Kilbreck?"

"You know why I was there. I had to be certain Abel and Marika were safe. I gave the Leprechauns my word I'd talk with you, and you'd help deal with the Cait."

I slung an arm around her shoulders, touched by her faith in me. It wasn't as if I could snap my fingers, and the Cait would do my bidding. "The Leprechauns can wait until I've had a shower. I won't have any luck displacing the Cait unless I muster an army."

"Or ask Earth to help."

"Not a sure thing but worth a shot." We'd reached our rooms. I opened the door with a thought.

"Something has to be," Abria was saying. "Those poor little things were soaked through. They need their home back."

The door shut behind us. I shucked clothes as I crossed to the bathroom. The little folk must have put on quite a show for Abria. They weren't nearly as helpless as they'd led her to believe.

Abria laughed merrily. "I have your number, bud. You're trying to divert me with your incredible body."

I turned and bowed. "Would madam care to join me in the shower?"

"Since the Leprechauns have to wait anyway, how can I say no?" In one fluid movement, she pulled her top over her head. The sight of firm, full breasts with their dollar-sized strawberry nipples drove everything else from my mind. My cock shot to fullness.

The fucking Leprechauns could indeed wait their turn. So could everyone else in the world. Odin's unmistakable laughter rolled through my mind.

"No wonder you wanted to keep that one to yourself," he chortled.

Why that sneaky bastard. He'd planted some kind of magical listening device or camera or something.

"What was that?" Abria stepped out of her trousers.

Unwilling to tell her we had an audience riding sidesaddle, I scooped her into my arms and herded us beneath a showerhead. "Nothing to worry about," I murmured. For now, I slapped up wards to defeat Odin's voyeurism. Later, I'd locate the damned bug—or whatever it was—and dismantle it. Meanwhile, he could curse his heart out in the background.

Water splashed off my chest. Abria wound her arms around me. Heedless of everything, I crashed my mouth over hers and drank her in.

CHAPTER 7
ABRIA

I was certain I'd heard something, but it could wait. The only important thing was Blake's body smushed against mine. We ended up with my legs wrapped around his hips and his arms beneath my thighs as he supported me. Soap, shampoo, and sex blended together.

During our early months together, we'd become champs at quickies in every situation imaginable. Dripping water and panting, he released inside me. Heat painted my vault with liquid lust. I'd already crested, but his passion pushed me over the edge once more.

Every nerve in my body was alight with passion and need. I sank my teeth into his shoulder and raked my nails up his back. The water shifted from steaming to tepid. Before it turned to ice, I reached around and pushed the tap to the off position.

"Why is it cold?" I was still struggling to get a straight breath into my sex-saturated body.

He licked a trail up my neck before lifting me off his cock and setting my feet on the marble floor. "Because you distract me."

I laughed. No hot water tanks here. He'd been using magic—until he was too absorbed in lovemaking not to. He ruffled my wet hair and tossed a thick white terrycloth towel in my direction.

Grabbing it, I blew him kisses and padded into the bedroom to find something dry to wear. When I heard his footsteps behind me, I asked, "So, where were you?"

"Hunting for Herne."

I stepped into a long denim skirt and boots but stopped tugging clothing on to give Blake my full attention. "Because of my dreams?" At his nod, I went on. "Did you find him?"

Blake shook his head. "Didn't even find anyone who'd seen him."

After pulling a black woolen shirt over my head and layering a fluffy blue vest over it, I perched on the edge of the bed. "If he's not alive, then why am I dreaming about him?"

"Never said he was dead," Blake commented.

"Yeah, but if you couldn't find him…"

"Probably means I didn't look in the right place. I did have a go round with Odin, though."

Oh-oh. Tucking my legs beneath me, I waited for more.

Blake slithered into buff-colored leather trousers and a white linen shirt embroidered with blue runes. He laced his feet into old-fashioned boots that reached to mid-calf. Every time he moved, he was grace incarnate; I could have watched him doing mundane tasks forever.

"I started in the Nine Worlds," he explained. "When I left there, I combed through the UK with no success. Since I hadn't been all that thorough with Odin's domain, I decided to return, except I changed my mind. When I got there, I redirected my spell, but Odin nabbed me before I could escape."

"Not liking the sound of that," I muttered.

Blake made a sour face. "Hel and her damned snakes showed up. When one of them headed for me, I nipped its intention in the bud. After that, I girded myself for a pitched battle. Never happened. Odin didn't want to do away with me. He's a bully, but he doesn't do much of anything that isn't well thought-out."

"Where'd the dead smell come from?"

"The Hunt showed up. Odin left after that, and so did I."

I turned my hands palms up. "That's all?"

"Not quite. He said Herne had never been to the Nine Realms, and I was wasting my time looking for him there."

"We're not going to solve that problem anytime soon," I said. "Let's see what we can do for the Leprechauns."

Blake smiled, walked toward me, and tilted my chin up with a forefinger. "They made quite an impression on you."

"I guess. I feel sorry for them. The Cait are nothing but a bunch of tyrants. At least they didn't displace anyone from their last set of caves."

"We don't know that," Blake pointed out. "Seals or sea lions probably lived there before."

"Well, they weren't paddling in the tide begging for their home back." I paused for a beat. "What can we do to help them? The Leprechauns, not sea life."

"Danu would be a far better choice—" Blake began.

The whoosh of wings and Hedrek's signature magical mixture bore down on me. Sure enough, the owl burst into the room in a shower of golden sparks. Before they totally cleared, the owl hooted, "Arianrhod says they're on their own."

"Really?" I frowned at the owl. "She wasn't willing to draw Danu into the loop?"

Hedrek ruffled his feathers. "I only stopped here to alert you. Need to return to watch over Abel and Marika."

"Hold up," Blake said. "What about Herne?"

The owl clacked his beak twice. "I think she knows... something, but she wasn't in a sharing mood. Something had her riled up. She barely gave me a nod before kicking me out of Caer Sidi."

"Not how she usually treats you," I murmured. "Any clue as to what's amiss?"

"If I knew, I'd have said so." Hedrek sounded miffed; perhaps it was catching.

Before I could question him further, he was gone. While I welcomed his concern for Abel and Marika, I'd have liked a shred more information about his field trip to Caer Sidi, except there didn't appear to be anything further to disclose.

"If she told him no," Blake said slowly, "the odds of us getting a different answer are remote."

"Do you have a better idea?" I settled my hands on my hips.

"Than?"

"Paying Arianrhod a visit ourselves."

"Not at the top of my list. Interacting with her when

she's in a decent mood isn't easy. From Hedrek's account, she'll probably kick us out as soon as she lays eyes on us. How about we start with Cailleach?"

Much as I liked the winter witch goddess, she was lower down the food chain. It meant she might be more inclined to hear us out, though.

"I'm game. Is there anything you need to do before we leave here?"

"Good point. Give me a few moments to locate Breanne and Kirwan."

"I'll be in the library," I told him.

He crossed the room and kissed me once, brief, intense, and full of promise. "Researching Leprechauns?" He asked after he'd raised his lips from mine.

"You know me too well."

"Aye, and I still adore you. Back soon." He strode from the room.

I followed but turned toward Underhill's vast compendium of books and scrolls. Borrowing a page from Breanne's tutelage, I visualized what I wanted to know. By the time I walked through high double doors leading into the library, the long table was littered with source material.

Magical tomes hold a draw unlike any other. I have no idea how much time passed before I heard Blake's tread approaching.

"Find anything?" he asked.

I held a scroll open with the flat of my hand and glanced his way. "Lots, but nothing that will help us. Apparently, Leprechauns have done a fine job of alienating both mortals and mages."

"It does complicate things," Blake agreed.

"You knew." I narrowed my eyes.

"Of course, I did."

"Mmph. No matter how many tricks they played on the unsuspecting, they didn't deserve to be kicked out of their home."

Blake perched on the edge of the table, facing me. "Probably not. But we can't allow ourselves to get sidetracked."

"What do you mean?" I moved my hand, and the scroll rolled itself into a tight cylinder.

"Once we displace the Cait, the Leprechauns' problem will go away. We can't force Danu to care about her minions. I'd like to locate Herne—if it's possible. Once we've done that, we can revisit the Leprechaun problem."

"But you have to visit them and explain what you have in mind," I told him.

"Why?" He arched both brows.

"Because I promised you would." I didn't bother to share the snide remarks that had accompanied my offer. Things like, *what good is he?*

Blake smiled indulgently. "Guess you eliminated any wiggle room, but I want to pay Cailleach a visit first."

"She might shed light on both problems," I mused. "Herne's location and rustling up Danu to help the little people."

"Herne is a maybe. Danu is probably a hard no. While powerful in her own right, Cailleach isn't a Celt. Means she wouldn't be privy to much of anything about their comings or goings. And Danu was always an enigma. Even her own people rarely see her."

"How do you know?" Genuinely curious, I focused on Blake.

"My information could be dated, but when the Celts roamed the Highlands, Danu was scarcely ever amongst them."

"Doesn't mean they didn't know where she was," I argued.

"Also doesn't mean they did," he shot back. "I heard plenty of grumbling back in the day, and she wasn't the only one her kin bitched about. The Morrigan was always stirring some shitpot or another. Arawn couldn't keep his dead in line. Gwydion was a sanctimonious ass. The list is long."

Fascinating. The Celts had always treated me like yesterday's trash, but I'd assumed they respected each other. "Not much we can do about their internecine squabbles. We have a plan. Ready to leave?"

"I am."

I chivvied the resource materials back to their respective spots on the library's vast shelf system. "Anything interesting from Kirwan or Breanne."

Blake shrugged. "Depends how you define interesting."

I was on my feet. The draw of Blake's magic pulled me toward him. I could have fought it, but I didn't want to. "Let me rephrase that." I leveled my gaze at him. "Do we have to do anything in particular on the home front?"

He shook his head. "Naught that won't keep. Mostly, Breanne and her generals are mapping out the next offensive against the Cait."

Blake's spell enveloped me and bore us out of Underhill.

"Can't you move them to a borderworld, or something?" I asked.

"Sure. Stopping them from moving back would be the problem." Breath hissed through Blake's teeth. "I can harness their power, but if I'm not there to ride herd on them, eventually, they'll garner enough to return from wherever we put them."

"Rotating guard duty?"

"I'd never get enough volunteers."

I kept my thoughts to myself and hoped Blake wasn't romping through my mind. Now that I knew more, it appalled me his subjects didn't treat him with more respect. He was more figurehead than actual leader—until the shit hit the fan, and then they dumped everything in his lap expecting him to fix it for them.

I slapped a lid on my annoyance. I'd never been responsible for more than a handful of animals. Even that had weighed heavy on me, heavy enough, I'd preferred to work alone. Blake had a system in place, one he'd honed over thousands of years. I'd be well-served to step back and trust he knew what he was doing.

A brisk salt breeze filled my nostrils. Moments later, the expanse of beach where we'd gotten married stretched around us. Birds shrieked, wheeling overhead as they spotted me and banked for landings. Seals lumbered from the surf.

"The welcoming committee knows you're here," Blake chuckled.

A pair of gulls landed on my shoulders. Ravens plopped down creating a circle around me. I settled on a flat rock, soaking up love. Most of these creatures had been at our wedding. Bleats and caws and grunts filled the marine air. I nuzzled and scratched and petted, at one with my world.

The ley lines had been convinced I belonged with them, but this was my place: in the midst of animals who adored me. Blake stood off to one side, multihued power creating a vortex around him.

He has many forms. This one was taller, broader, and more commanding. Black wings spread to both sides as he shaped magic to do his bidding. I'd never witnessed the full spectrum of his ability, and I hoped I never did for it would mean our very existence was on the line.

The ocean swirled and churned. Cailleach rose from the waves and skimmed along their tops as she made her way to shore. Half a head taller than me with a spare, bony build, she had pronounced cheekbones, a high forehead, and a squared-off chin. A beak of a nose dominated her rough features. Tangled silver hair hung to her knees. Dressed in one of her many robes—this one a faded violet—she looked like witches portrayed in children's books.

One moment, she rode the waves. The next, she pushed between two seals and a hawk to drape an arm around my shoulders. "What a pleasure, child."

Blake sheathed his power, reverting to his more familiar form. He strode close. "Good to see you, goddess."

She inclined her head. "You as well, Sidhe, but I'm confused. Most newly mated couples don't leave their marriage bed for the first century or so. Have you tired of one another so soon?" Thick gray brows knit together. "Is that why you've come? For a love charm or two?"

"Oh my no. Abria and I are more than fine."

"I wish we could stay in bed and eat bonbons," I cut in, "but our problems didn't go away because we married."

Cailleach flapped a hand. "Pfft. The Cait are an annoyance. Surely, the rest of the Sidhe can dispatch them elsewhere."

"Would that it were so simple," Blake muttered.

"Have you seen Herne lately?" I blurted. May as well get our agenda out on the table.

The witch goddess drew back and stared at me. "Herne? Did I hear you right, child?"

I really didn't like her calling me that, but it was splitting hairs on my part. "Yeah, you heard right. I've been dreaming about a golden stag and Becca and riding to war. Birgit is convinced the stag means I'm dreaming of the Wild Hunt."

"I didn't make the connection right away," Blake admitted.

Cailleach withdrew the arm around my shoulders and held up a hand. "Hold up. Tell me everything. Start at the beginning."

I did, with Blake inserting the odd bit here and there. It didn't take all that long. When I was done, I waited to see what Cailleach's take was.

She hopped off the flat rock where I sat and shooed a few seals back to clear a patch of wet earth. Once it was done, power flowed from her fingers until a glowing white pentagram took shape. I'd spent enough time learning from her, I understood she was seeking information from her guides.

I'd never figured out who they were, but she used them about as often as she used her library.

While Cailleach communed with spirits, I wandered among the animals ringed around us soaking in their purity of heart. After a time, Blake joined me. Having him by my side, sharing my world, felt right. The animals accepted him in much the same way they did me, but the Sidhes' link to the natural world is part of their magic.

The sun had moved from midheaven to hovering above the western horizon when Cailleach looked up from the pentagram. Its inner light faded; its markings soaked into the sand.

When she crooked a finger our way, we joined her.

"First off," she began, addressing Blake, "I was never privy to the trick that spirited you through my gates to another world. Once it happened, I tried to undo it, but the Celts had you locked away where I couldn't intervene." She made a sour face. "I hate to admit it, but they're still stronger than I am."

"Good to know," Blake murmured. "I was going to bring it up but decided to let it slide. It was in the past, and it didn't cause any lasting damage."

"Only because you got yourself out of there," Cailleach countered. "You are correct about it being in the past, though. Far more important is the present. And the future."

"Do you believe the stag in my vision is Herne?" I pressed.

"Probably."

"Do you know where to find him?" Blake spoke up.

"Not sure. I need to ask a few folk."

"My thought was he means to wrest the Hunt from Odin," Blake went on. "He always resented giving up the helm. Word of Abria's enhanced power could have reached him, and—"

"Hold up." Cailleach's words carried a sharp edge. "Until we know more, you gain naught by conjecture." She looked from one to the other of us. "Is Herne the only reason you sought me out?"

"Not exactly," I mumbled.

"Out with it, child. We don't have all day."

I smiled. In the two years I'd spent learning from her, she'd used that phraseology frequently.

Blake stepped in. "The Cait moved beneath Ben Kilbreck."

Cailleach turned a hand palm up. "What about the Leprechauns? Where's Danu in all this?"

"Same question we're asking," Blake said. "Do you know how to alert Danu her people need her?"

Light was leaching from the day. The sky traded leaden gray for deep purple as the sun dropped below the horizon and faded from view.

"Maybe. You've given me much to do. Return in two days' time. If Fate smiles on my efforts, I will have answers for you."

I opened my mouth to thank her, but she was gone.

Blake cobbled a spell together and motioned for me to join him. I tapped into it and said, "Hold up, there."

"What? Why? We're returning to Underhill. No reason to wait here for two days."

I shook my head. "Nope. We're going to reassure the Leprechauns we're working on solving their problem."

Blake viewed it as a waste of time. I saw as much blazoned across his mind. To his credit, he switched up his casting, and said, "Whatever milady desires," and shepherded us to the Highlands.

"You know," I whispered into his ear, "I've always fancied a tryst in one of those creepy old castles."

"Would that be before or after the Leprechauns?" He reached around me to fondle a breast.

"After. If we show up reeking of sex, they'll never take us seriously."

"They probably won't anyway, but I admire your tenacity."

I laughed as the bulk of Ben Kilbreck took shape in front of us. "That's me," I agreed, "the original stubborn bitch."

"You're perfect, darling. Never change a thing. Come on, let's get this part over and done with."

"For now. It won't be don't until they have their home back."

"Good timing." Hedrek flew toward us. "Trouble's brewing, and I could use assistance."

My heart sank. So much for wild abandoned fucking in a musty old castle. The owl never requested support. Whatever this was must be pretty bad.

"Tell us," Blake was saying. "Everything."

"The cats are in trouble. I can't get them out."

Crap. Crap. Crap. Not thinking, just reacting, I sprinted for the opening to Ben Kilbreck.

CHAPTER 8
BLAKE

What the unholy fuck? I didn't want to yell after Abria—besides, she wouldn't have stopped—so I caught her midstride with magical netting. It would infuriate her, but it was better than her racing in there half-cocked and ruining any coordinated rescue effort.

When she flipped around to face me, her cheeks were the same shade as her hair. I'd have reeled her closer, but no reason to toss fat on the flames. Pelting forward, I dropped a hand on each shoulder and released my casting.

"What do you think you're doing?" I put steel in my tone.

"What the fuck does it look like?" Abria writhed beneath my grasp. "Let go of me, goddammit."

"If you promise not to do anything stupid."

"It was not stupid. I'm responsible for them, and—"

"You can't go in there alone," Hedrek hooted. "I barely

got out. They know someone was inside, but weren't able to catch me." He raised a wing displaying a long, ugly cut along his ribs. It was closing over as we watched, but the feathers beneath were clotted with blood.

"Did any drip?" I demanded.

"Don't think so. I was careful," the owl replied.

"So what if it did?" Abria snarled. "It's not like the Cait are bright enough to figure anything out."

I tightened my hold on her. "Never underestimate them. They're arrogant, but more than capable of smelling Celtic magic on Hedrek."

"Good." Abria rubbed her hands together. "Maybe they'll assume Danu is on her way to kick them out."

I hadn't considered that possibility. Having them rattled and on the defensive could work in our favor. "What's happening with Abel and Marika?" I asked the owl. If we were going to effect a rescue, I needed details.

He dropped his wing to his side. The nasty gash had mostly healed. "I began watching from outside. It was adequate last time I was here. When I couldn't sense them anymore, I went in."

"And?" Blake prodded.

"It's a mess in there. The energy is even more fragmented than when I was last here. I started in the spots the Cait don't frequent, probably because they're brimming with Celtic magic."

He fluffed his feathers. "The higher you go inside the mountain, the more Celtic enchantment bears down on you. Starting at the top, I worked my way from level to level until I was in the tunnel system running beneath Ben Kilbreck."

The feathers around his beak crinkled with disgust. "The odor is indescribable. Why they don't do something about it is beyond me."

"Did you find Abel and Marika?" Abria's voice shrilled. I let go of her, and she rolled her shoulders this way and that.

"Finally. They're in a cage two levels down from the entrance. I showed myself to them and took a crack at the lock with my beak."

"Why not magic?" Abria demanded.

"If I had, the Cait would have come on a dead run. They're not so far gone they wouldn't react to strange magic in their midst." He hooted softly. "When I couldn't crack the lock, I tried to form a travel spell to rescue them. It wouldn't reach through the metal. That was when I knew I needed help."

"Did you find out why they'd been imprisoned?" I asked.

Hedrek nodded. "The Cait held another vote after Abel and Marika returned. It was close but went against the cats. The current plan is to use them as hostages or bait to draw you"—he stared at me—"close enough to parley."

It made sense. They were outnumbered and running out of places to settle. I could pardon them, but why in the goddess's name would I?

They assume I hope the best for every Sidhe. I answered my own question. I hadn't hung them out to dry when they defected, so why would I hesitate to welcome them now?

They were truly delusional if they believed I'd forgive and forget their many transgressions.

"At least the cats are safe for the moment," Abria gritted.

"If they need them as bait, they'll keep them alive, but we have to get them out of there."

"I'll take care of it."

"How?" She narrowed her eyes.

"By making them think I'll offer clemency, but only if they release the cats as a show of good faith."

"Brilliant." Hedrek hooted with enthusiasm. "They're egotistical enough to fall for it."

I wasn't certain of that. "We need to think this through. I can't waltz in there and admit I planted the cats as spies. They don't know we were present when their last den imploded."

"Got it." Abria spoke up. "Use my link as an excuse. Tell them I sensed my charges were miserable, being held against their will, and we've come to investigate."

I rolled it around, trying it out. "Might work," I said.

She mock punched me in the side. "How about, dazzling idea, darling."

"Aye, that too." I paused for a beat. "For this to be believable, you'll have to enter with me."

"It's dangerous for her." Hedrek clacked his beak in protest. "She killed their last leader. They'll not have forgotten."

"Tough shit," I growled. "I still hold power over them. Not a lot and not for long, but enough to get us in and out."

"I'll be close." Hedrek spread his wings and perched on a boulder near the bulk of the mountain.

Abria hooked a hand beneath my elbow. "Let's get this done."

If she was still angry with me for foiling her forward charge, it was fading.

"Let me do the talking at first," I cautioned.

She snorted. "What you mean is to not let my temper out of its cage. I'll do my best, but I hate those fuckers."

"None too fond of them myself."

Together, we walked through the nearest opening into Ben Kilbreck. I stopped once we cleared the rounded lintel and shouted, "Sentry. To me." For now, they were still my subjects, and I'd be every inch their regent.

A Cait scuttled out of shadows, started to bow to me, but recovered fast. "What do you want?" he snarled.

This was a good time to play dumb. Even though I knew full well, I asked, "Who leads the Cait these days?"

"Zottre." The Cait's reply was sullen.

"Find him." Spreading my wings, I made myself tall, imposing.

"No need. I'm right here."

Zottre walked purposely toward us. His pale hair was braided close to his head. His brows formed question marks. His chin was pointed, as were his ears. Amber eyes with vertical slit pupils sat above slanted cheekbones. Like most of the Cait, he was naked. When you shift frequently, garments are an impediment.

"She must leave." Zottre jerked his chin at me.

"She is my mate," I thundered. "And your queen. Show some respect."

His pale skin turned even whiter. Clearly, he hadn't expected my response.

"We are here," I continued, "on Abria's behalf. As you

know, she is an animal mage. She sensed two of her own being held against their will. Release them immediately."

Zottre's features took on a crafty aspect. "What's in it for the Cait if we do?"

"A bigger question is what happens to the Cait if you don't," I shot back.

"Now, now, boys." Abria squeezed my arm. "Release my cats as a show of good faith. And then I'm certain my mate will be more open to negotiating with you."

"Not without promises," Zottre sneered.

"What kind of promises?" I asked, well aware of what he had in mind.

"We return to Underhill." Amber eyes drilled into mine.

"Pfft. Just like that? You wreak havoc, turn against the rest of the Sidhe, and expect instant forgiveness?"

"Aye."

It took everything in me not to haul off and punch him. The crunch of bones wouldn't come close to assuaging my fury, but it might be a start. I adopted what I hoped was a neutral expression and said, "I'll need to confer with the council."

"Fine. The cats will still be here when you return."

Abria shook her head. "Nope. Not going to work that way. If you don't free Abel and Marika immediately, Blake won't be lifting a finger for you."

"Arrogant bitch." Zottre spat the words. "Stay out of this. You're not one of us. Hell, you're naught but an upstart mage who ruined magic for the rest of us."

"*Us* never included the Sidhe," I reminded him. "Don't

sling a load of solidarity crap around, either. The Cait have never given a shit for anyone beyond your catty selves."

Abria simpered sweetly. "Where have you been, Zottre? Your information is dated. I fixed that little problem. The ley lines are not only whole, but I am also part of them."

She took on an otherworldly glow so bright I shielded my eyes.

It didn't slow Zottre down one whit. "If I release the cats, it will bind you to plead our case before the Sidhe council."

"Only if I give you my word, which I already did. You have five minutes to produce the cats. If you do not, our business with you is finished. You will face the full wrath of the Sidhe army. This time, we won't stop until the last Cait is annihilated."

"But we're your people."

"Used to be," I corrected. "You're down to four minutes."

I'd taken a harsh stance, but I had something he wanted far more than two alley cats. I felt the zing of power as he sent orders telepathically. Moments later, Abel and Marika tore into the room yowling and hissing.

Abria scooped them into her arms and stormed out of the grotto beneath Ben Kilbreck.

I turned to follow her.

"When will I hear from you?" Zottre came as close to whining as I'd ever heard him.

"Sooner rather than later." He'd figure out he'd been played. Not today, but eventually.

"Don't be like that. I said we're sorry."

I kept walking. Sorry doesn't cut it when you've stepped as far out of line as my Cait Sidhe kinsmen.

The first breath of fresh air was sweet after the rank stench of the Cait's lair. Abria stood next to Hedrek with the cats cradled against her. A travel spell hovered around them. I stepped into it.

"I wasn't certain he'd go for it," Abria was saying as she told Hedrek what had happened.

"I boxed him in. He didn't really have any choice," I explained.

"Aye, if he'd done aught else, he'd have signed his people's death warrant," Hedrek hooted.

"It's already signed and sealed," I muttered. "He just doesn't know it yet."

"Thank you for getting us out of there," Abel said.

"We were ready to leave," Marika seconded.

"Even if you hadn't been, I'd have insisted," Abria told them. "Back to Inverness with you. Catch mice, grow fat, and regale the next generation with tales of your bravery."

Hedrek's spell dropped us in a dank alley. Assorted drunks in varying stages of inebriation scattered like a pack of rats. I should have asked earlier, but I said, "Before you go, did you garner information that might help us?"

"We were going to tell you." Abel squirmed in Abria's arms. She set him and Marika down.

"They can still get inside Underhill," Marika mewled.

"In their cat bodies," Abel added.

"Before they settled on the idea to use us as bait," Marika went on, "they were going to enter Underhill many times."

"Why many times?" I asked. Usually battles were won—or lost—soon after they were launched. It was particularly true for battles powered by magic. None of them ever dragged on like human conflagrations.

"They planned to take things, maybe a lot of things," Abel cut in.

Ugh. I squeezed my eyes shut and made a face. When I opened them, I asked, "Have they taken anything yet?"

"Not that we know of," Marika said.

"They're not very organized," Abel added. "Much talk, little agreement or initiative."

Marika howled plaintively. "They wouldn't survive a week here. Not as cats. Even a small group of rats could take them out."

"What are they after?" Abria arched a russet brow.

"Same question I had," the owl hooted.

"Objects in the council chamber," I said. "We have crystals and wands and gemstones that augment power. After that, their next target would be the armory. Powerful weapons reside there, blades that have never lost a skirmish."

I needed to return to Underhill and launch an inventory. Before we left, I crouched until I was at eye level with the cats. "Did you overhear anything else useful?"

They shook their heads, whiskers twitching.

I adopted a formal tone. "You did well. Thank you for your service to my people. I shall never forget your courage, and if you ever have need of aught, you've only to ask. If it's within my power, I'll grant whatever boon you'd like."

The cats raced away from us, bursting out the head of the alleyway and howling up a storm.

"Sneaky on the part of the Cait," Abria observed.

"That's them," I mumbled sourly. "Devious bastards."

"They'd have removed key elements supporting your defense," Hedrek said.

"Exactly. They have no chance of winning in a fair contest, so they found a way to even the odds."

The worst part was we'd never have known until it was too late. No one checked on our array of artifacts—or weapons. We assumed they wouldn't be disturbed.

No more. Those idyllic days had just crashed into a solid wall.

"Are you coming with us?" Abria asked the owl.

"You're returning to Underhill, right?" The owl fanned the air with outstretched wings.

"Yeah," Abria said. "We have at least a day left before we return to Cailleach."

"What's there?" Hedrek glanced from one to the other of us.

"Hopefully information about Herne," Abria answered.

"I'll take another crack at Arianrhod," Hedrek said. "Perhaps she'll be in a better mood."

Abria slung an arm around his feathered back crushing a wing feather or two in the process. The owl didn't rebuke her or flinch. "Take care, dear heart. Find us in Underhill once you're done."

Flapping lazily, he rose into the late afternoon sky.

"Anything you need in Nairn?" I asked.

"Nope. Not a thing, but there is a bed there, and more privacy than we're likely to see for quite some time."

I laughed. "Sold, wench."

"That's all it took?" She was laughing too. "Geez. You men are soooo weak."

"Any bloke would be lost confronted by your charms." I bowed low before adopting my human glamour. In case someone who wasn't drunk traipsed past, I didn't want to give them a coronary.

"Why you silver-tongued devil, you." She made a grab for my crotch.

I swathed us in magic and aimed for the second story of her home in Nairn.

CHAPTER 9
ABRIA

We sprawled in a sodden panting heap on my bed with Blake on top of me, cock still sunk into my body. What had begun during our travel spell burst into flames as we grappled with one another's clothing. We didn't have to remove much. For once, I wore long skirts. Easy enough to hike them out of the way, kneel, and shake my booty.

Blake's never been one to let an opportunity slide past, not when sex is on the table. I'd already freed his cock from his trousers. He knew precisely where it belonged.

The tail end of a series of orgasms buzzed around my body. I wriggled out from under him and lay on my side. Reaching between us, I stroked his tantalizingly thick appendage. "What I want," I announced, "is a solid week where we can do whatever we want. No distractions. No disturbances. No wars. No council nattering on about this or that. No Cait prima donnas."

He cupped the side of my face. "We had exactly that, darling, and you kicked me out of this very flat."

"That was different." I made a wry face.

"Oh really? How?"

"We weren't married then."

His striking features took on a thoughtful look. "If I'd asked you to marry me then, you'd have said no."

"You don't know that."

"Aye, but I do. You wanted your old life back more than you wanted me."

He was right, but I'd never give him the satisfaction of letting him know. "About that week..."

"I promise you we'll have it and more. Once we're past all the rest of this."

"But that could take centuries."

He shrugged. "So? We live forever. What difference does it make?"

I ran my fingertips down his face like a blind woman memorizing the planes of his cheeks, forehead, chin. I'd been a fool to chase him out of my life shortly after we met. He was my destiny. I knew it now. Why had I fought against it before?

"Abria?"

"Um-hum?"

"We need to get back to Underhill."

I dragged myself away from the special world the two of us created. "You're worried."

"Aye, I am. We've never kept an eye on any of our artifacts or our weapons. Why would we? Underhill modulates who can enter."

The pleasant sex haze retreated. "I'm sorry we didn't mete out more damage that night at Rait Castle."

"Goes double for me, but we can't go back."

"Can you really wipe them out and live with yourself?"

A heartrending sigh burbled from him. "Do I have a choice? I can't forgive them. I don't trust them. The only reason they're playing nice is they know they can't win in an all-out confrontation."

Blake shook dark hair out of his eyes and rolled to a sit. "If I capitulate—like they're expecting—and allow them back into the Sidhe realm, they'll bide their time, grow strong, and be in a much better position to conquer from within. Can't take that chance."

"Will the council agree?" I left the bed and made my way to my small bathroom. Wetting a washcloth, I cleaned myself up, rinsed it, and tossed it to Blake.

I'm not sure. Some will. Others view being a Sidhe as an exclusive club. Either you're in or you're out. No matter how damaged the Cait are, they're still Sidhe."

"You could have dissension among the ranks." I checked my garments. They were crinkled but otherwise serviceable. No need to change until I got back to Underhill.

"Not could, will."

"Do you have to tell them the Cait requested clemency?"

"What do you think?" He angled his head to one side and set his clothing to rights. We'd been so desperate for one another, we hadn't bothered to remove our shoes.

"If you don't, and they find out, there'll be hell to pay," I mumbled.

"Exactly. Ready to leave?"

I wasn't. Once I'd let my defenses crumble, I resented everything that got between Blake and me. It was stupid. Unrealistic. Small, petty, and selfish. It wasn't the person I wanted to be. I walked into his arms. "Ready. If there's any way I can help inventory things, let me know."

"Best thing you can do is research Herne. Damn it." He pounded a fist into his open palm. "We forgot to talk with the Leprechauns."

So we had. It was why we'd gone there in the first place.

"I can do that," I told him. "Meet you back at Underhill."

"Are you certain?"

"Very. The only reason they were expecting you is because I kicked that door open. It will be okay."

"What will you tell them?"

"That we're working on locating Danu."

He held onto me. "No heroics."

"Relax. I'm not going back into Ben Kilbreck. I'll just rustle up a Leprechaun or two, tell them we're working on fixing their problem, and leave. I'll only be a few minutes behind you returning to Underhill."

"I'll hold you to it." He let go of me and floated upward with outstretched wings. Before he collided with the ceiling, he vanished.

I prepared to leave too. One of these days, I'd move a few more of my things to Underhill, but it wasn't a priority. The Sidhe stronghold had an extensive wardrobe room with garments dating back a thousand years. Magic kept them from moldering to dust, and, from my limited observation, no one pilfered from the common stocks except me.

The Leprechauns had intimated each had an assigned

territory in the Highlands. Did their regions extend as far south as Nairn? Maybe I wouldn't have to travel all the way to Ben Kilbreck.

A glance out my dirty window convinced me to trade my skirt for trousers. It was pouring with no letup in sight. A few moments later, garbed in black twill pants, stout boots, and a rain jacket, I walked down the steep stairs and out into the storm locking the door behind me. Wind howled and slapped me with fat, chilly raindrops. I dragged a hood over my head and cinched it tight.

Hunched against the gale, I headed for the site that had once held Nairn Castle. It wasn't far. I hoped to find a Leprechaun or two in the catacombs beneath its ruins, but luck wasn't with me. My next stop was Cawdor Castle. MacBeth's fictional home, it was built around 1380. Unlike Nairn Castle, this one had been renovated many times, was still standing and a major tourist attraction.

I'd assumed the little people would have been more drawn to a deserted locale; I'd been wrong. As I blended in with crowds of tourists gawking at the imposing structure and waiting for tours to begin, I sensed enchantment zinging off battlements.

I should have begun this task warded. Transitioning to invisibility wasn't prudent, not in the middle of this many people. Crap. Why didn't the rain bother them? Gliding out of the line I'd been standing in, I circled around toward the rear of Cawdor.

Until my route was blocked by an imposing gate. Whoever ran this show didn't want tourists wandering about unchaperoned. No one stood anywhere near; I summoned warding and jumped the iron gate. On the far side, I raised my mind voice and hoped someone would come running.

Or walking. I wasn't particular.

A Brownie poked her head out of a hole I hadn't noticed next to the courtyard wall. The rest of her blocky body followed. Maybe a meter high, she was as broad as she was tall. Brown curls framed her features; brown eyes regarded me with mild interest. She wore a beige robe spun from rough fabric. Shaking a finger my way, she shrilled, *"You're not supposed to do that."*

"Do what?"

"Toss magic about."

I shrugged. *"Mortals can't see me. I need to speak with a Leprechaun."*

The Brownie bristled. *"Why not me? I'm as good as them."*

I bit back a sigh. I'd forgotten about the longstanding rivalry between them. *"Of course, you are,"* I agreed. *"But I still need a Leprechaun. Are any of them here?"*

"They left. So, it's me or nothing." She puffed out her chest like an angry chicken.

"Do you know when they'll return?"

"They don't report to me."

Damn it. No point wasting more time here. I had turned to leave when I heard, *"Danu's going to slay you alive for lying, Mari."*

Footsteps pattered my way. I flipped back around to see two Leprechauns trotting toward me. Excellent. My day was looking up.

I knelt and waited until they reached me. *"I bear messages from Elwyn Cardassier."*

"Why isn't he here himself?" one Leprechaun asked.

"He is deep in consultation with the Sidhe council about the Cait problem."

"Mmph," the other Leprechaun muttered. *"Can't see how it affects him much."*

"It does." I aimed for reassuring. *"He accepts full responsibility for what they've done to you—and others. He couldn't be here, but he sent me to assure you we're looking for Danu and figuring out how to force the Cait from your home."*

When they didn't respond, I added, *"Will you please let the rest of your people know?"*

After a long pause, both nodded. *"How can we find Elwyn?"* the Brownie asked. Sheesh. I'd nearly forgotten about her.

"He's in Underhill."

"But we can't go there," one of the Leprechauns protested.

"If you present at one of the gates, someone will come." They didn't appear mollified, so I added, *"I'm certain Danu will address this."*

The Leprechauns laughed uproariously as if I'd told a very funny joke. When I could get a word in edgewise, I asked, *"Is there something I'm not aware of?"*

No one answered. The Brownie popped back into her hidey hole. The Leprechauns ran along the side of the castle and disappeared. Presumably down another hole.

I stared after them, flummoxed. Had I done enough? Or did I still need to show up closer to Ben Kilbreck?

"Stop right there," a male voice boomed.

Fuck. Crap. Shit. I'd let my ward slip to converse with the little people. A constable stood on the far side of the fence glaring my way. I wasn't in the mood to lie my way out of how I'd defeated the gate.

He stepped closer. "Abria. Is that you?"

Damn. Damn. Damn. Could this get any worse? He must know me from my private detective business. Power flowed from me. I circled his mind and erased the last few minutes. He shuffled backward, ready for a do over. While he was still disoriented, I jumped the hell out of there. Lesson learned. Never wield magic close to where I live.

Not that I still lived in Nairn, but my erstwhile home was there.

Hoping my conversation with the little folk would percolate down through the ranks, I instructed my travel spell to take me to Underhill.

"No good deed goes unpunished," I muttered under my breath as the earthy home of the Sidhe took shape around me.

What should I do next? Three choices. Library, Blake's rooms, or the council chamber. The first two were safe enough. The third hit-or-miss. Most of the Sidhe didn't exactly accept me. They'd grudgingly accorded me points when I outlined a more effective way to deal with the Cait, but it hadn't earned me much. I felt certain they'd rather Blake had married within their ranks—or better yet, not at all.

I wanted the satisfaction of going where I pleased, being as in-your-face as I could, but it was juvenile. And it would cause problems for Blake. He wasn't the type of regent where his subjects did whatever he said. Far from it. Mostly, he was on the receiving end of tons of pushback.

Me popping into the council meeting wouldn't help anyone but me.

I stopped midstride as understanding bit deep. It wouldn't help me, either. Blake's people needed time to get used to me. I didn't need to be subservient or fawning, but forcing my way into everything wouldn't endear me to anyone.

Blake would tolerate it because he's smitten, but I needed to pull my head out of my ass. Part of the problem was I'd never lived with anyone. Not since I escaped the Celts centuries ago. And that wasn't exactly "living with" them since they chucked me in a cave and forgot about me.

Food and water showed up regularly, but no one ever stayed to ask how I was or if I needed anything. Those first twenty years or so had been wretched; I'd blocked them out of my mind.

For the most part.

My beginnings hadn't prepared me for much of anything but keeping to myself. I headed for the library. I could do our cause more good by finding out about Herne.

Maybe the stag in my dreams every night wasn't him but an actual magical stag. It wasn't beyond the pale. All animals are drawn to me. Why not this one?

But what about the Hunt connection?

Don't know if there is one, I answered myself. It had been Birgit's first take, but she could have been mistaken.

On my way to the library, I stopped in the doorway. Reading material about Herne had plopped obligingly on the long table, but I might be better served outdoors hunting for the stag in my dreams.

Because the idea plunked into my mind unbidden, it was probably the proper course. I glanced at the books and scrolls, pages riffling invitingly, and told them, "Stay put. I'll be back later."

As if they understood, they quieted. I blinked a time or two, not believing they were that sentient. And then, I turned and left. This time, I walked out of Underhill rather than powering my egress with magic. I probably should have left Blake a note or something, but I didn't plan to be gone all that long.

I passed gateways, each zapping me as I walked through. Presumably, if I'd been a foe, Underhill's power would have cut me in two. Finally, I reached a familiar stairway. It spit me out in Rait Castle's courtyard.

The transition from Underhill to Earth is always a surprise. For some reason, I'd expected it would still be daytime. It wasn't. Clear dark skies rode overhead with a sliver of a moon and a million points of light.

I stopped and stared for a few minutes. Clear evenings are a rarity in the Highlands. I was determined to enjoy this one. The night might be clear, but it was cold. I was underdressed, so I made up the difference with a slight flow of power.

While I was gazing upward, familiar hoofbeats cantered my way. A smile split my lips. Becca. I hadn't seen the unicorn since my wedding, and we hadn't had much time to visit then.

"Feel like a ride?" The unicorn nudged me with her glistening silver horn.

I swung onto her back. "Sure, but we have a task," I informed her.

"What might that be?" She trotted away from the castle and into nearby woods.

"I seek a stag with golden horns. Have you seen such a creature?"

Becca stopped so abruptly, I almost went over her head. "You do not want to cross paths with him." She punctuated her words with a shrill neigh.

"Why not? Who is he? And where have you come across him?"

Becca started off at a sedate pace. I sensed nervous energy coursing through her, which was highly unusual. Most unicorns are unflappable. They're the executioners in mage-land. The only creatures who can end immortal lives.

"You must abandon this task." Her usually melodious voice took on a somber tone.

We threaded our way through trees and shrubbery. Trees were unusual this far north. They had a tough time growing at this latitude, and the original ones had been chopped down hundreds of years ago to make dwellings or fires.

Since Becca didn't seem inclined to add to her warning, I said, "You've known me for a long time. While I respect your judgment, you telling me to leave off something I deem critical won't be enough until you back it up with facts."

"Why is finding the stag critical?"

At least she was willing to hear me out, so I sketched a

composite of the dreams that plagued my slumber almost every night.

The quality of the forest shifted. We had to be in another world. Trees like these with orange and violet leaves and white trunks didn't grow on Earth. She stopped in the center of a grove. Treetops towered a hundred meters over our heads.

"Get down. It is safe to talk here."

I'd been right about us leaving Earth. "Where are we?"

"The unicorns' border world."

I'd had no idea such a place existed. "Thank you for trusting me with knowledge of your—"

"Save your breath. I'll scrub your mind of its location before we return."

I tossed a leg over her back and slid to the ground. No handy sitting rocks were within eyesight. But then, unicorns didn't spend any time sitting.

Becca hoofed around until she faced me. "He's trying to get to you," she said. "You must not allow it. I'll instruct Blake to strengthen the protections around Underhill. He's sneaky, that one. Still, I'm surprised he broke through Faery's existing defenses."

It was almost as if she were talking to herself. I waited through a few more sentences along the same lines before I asked. "Who are we talking about here? Is it Herne? Or is the stag just a stag and not a man wearing a glamour?"

A shrill whinny was followed by two more so loud my ears rang. "You spent years with Cailleach," Becca hissed. "Years. Did she teach you nothing?"

Fuck me. My temper has always been a liability.

Shouting at the unicorn wouldn't help. Neither would launching my own travel spell and hotfooting it back to Underhill.

It took self-discipline, but I asked, "What would she have taught me that's relevant to my current problem?"

Becca tapped me with her horn. A jolt of unicorn enchantment romped through my brain none too gently. "You really don't know," she muttered.

I unclenched my jaws. "If I did, I wouldn't have asked you. Damn it, Becca. I'm not a game-player. I asked because I need information. Blake and I face many problems. If my dreams turn out to be prophetic—and it's likely since I have them every night—I need to figure out why I'm at the head of an army, who my enemies are—beyond the Cait—and where the stag figures in all of this."

I paused to take a breath and forged ahead. "You're in that dream too. I'm astride you, and the stag rides with us."

"Not in any universe," she huffed.

"Okay. Fine. But please, please tell me what you know."

Another horn tap. "On one condition."

I started to say *anything*, but reeled that reply in quickly. "What is it?"

"You must not use the knowledge to find the stag."

Breath streamed from my nostrils, creating clouds in the chilly air. "I'm not sure I can make that promise. The best I can do is try. May I tell Blake whatever you impart?"

After a long pause, she nodded.

While she was considering my question about Blake, I came up with another concession that might free her lips. "What I can promise is Blake and I will include you—and other unicorns if you'd like—in any discussions about the stag."

I waited, gazing into Becca's dark, liquid eyes.

Finally, she said, "I'm not happy, but it will do. Let me tell you a story. It has its beginnings long ago when the world was young and those like me revealed ourselves to humankind..."

CHAPTER 10
BLAKE

It took a while to rustle up all the council members. I didn't blame them for dragging their feet. We'd had more council meetings in the last few months than we'd had since the 1500s when the Dark Fae went on a rampage. While some council members like Kirwan and Breanne wanted an active say in our strategies, many others would have preferred for me to simply fix things.

Wave a wand and force the Cait into line. Preferably without any mess or bloodletting.

The longer we talked, the clearer it became I'd been correct in my assumption that cutting the knees out from beneath our Cait kinsmen left a bad taste in a whole lot of mouths.

"Didn't you say they apologized?" someone groused.

"Aye, should be good enough," another agreed. "Everyone makes mistakes, and—"

"Mistakes?" I thundered. "Mistakes? Oberon's balls,

man, they tried to take over Underhill. The only reason the plan failed was because I sniffed it out before it came full circle."

"But they've seen the error of their ways," a woman called out.

"If you believe that, I bet you believe mirrors are gateways into Underhill," I retorted.

She reddened, muttered, "This didn't use to be an autocracy," and stormed out of the room.

Eh, she had a point. I've never been one for slinging power about, but it was precisely what I'd been doing ever since convening this meeting. I took a different tack. "Does anyone here actually trust the Cait? As in, name one Cait you trust implicitly."

Silence sat heavy in the chamber.

I turned my hands palms up. "I don't trust them either. They can float pretty words when they're cornered with no viable options. The first decade or so would probably slide past without incident if they moved back to their old quarters in Underhill. Eventually, though, they'd leverage their position to sabotage from within."

"You can't know that," the one who'd insisted they'd apologized argued.

"Neither can you know it's not so," I shot back. "Why take the chance? We may not always get along, but when misfortunes befall, I have faith in each of you to do your part to maintain Sidhe integrity."

I waited. No one said anything, so I tossed out more thoughts. "'Tisn't as if it was only one defection. The Cait have been chipping away at their goal for years."

"What goal?" someone called out.

I resisted throttling her. Or asking where she'd been while we were deep in defending ourselves. "Their goal is quite clear," I told her. "They believe they should be the overlords here and the rest of us their minions."

"Did they tell you that?" Autocracy woman was back and had found her tongue.

"Not in so many words, but their actions are clear." I splayed both hands on a large crystal that sat in front of me on the dais. It quivered and took on a soft blue glow. I absorbed peace from its vibrations.

"'Tisn't necessary for all of you to fight," I went on, "but if you wish to sit this one out, please do so quietly. No aid to our enemy."

"But they're part of us," the woman protested.

"They used to be," I corrected her. "No more. We're moving on here. Anyone who doesn't want to be involved in this planning process is free to leave."

I glanced around the room establishing eye contact with everybody. Amid throat clearing and hemming and hawing, no one actually stood and walked out.

First hurdle, accomplished. Crap. It had taken over an hour to achieve even this rudimentary level of consensus. Where was Abria? She should have been back by now. I reached for her with my mind and ran into a blank wall.

Not only not here, but also nowhere close.

"Elwyn?" Kirwan nudged me.

I nodded at him. Abria had been taking care of herself for most of her life. I might be worried about her, but like as not she was fine. She had more than enough magic and ingenuity to get herself out of most thorny situations. When I'd raced into the bowels of Hell to rescue her, she told me to get lost and extricated herself—with the help of a few rats and ravens.

"Thanks for your support," I told everyone but stopped shy of fawning or telling them how much I appreciated them not fleeing for the hills at the first hint of trouble.

"The Cait are holed up beneath Ben Kilbreck," I went on. "Bands of pissed off Leprechauns are roaming the Highlands bemoaning being ousted from their home."

"Danu should be the one to step in," Kirwan said firmly.

"She isn't," I told him. "Besides, while the Leprechauns are her charges, the Cait are ours." I almost said mine but wanted to stress inclusivity. I couldn't dance on two floors. Either we went to war as a cohesive group, or Abria and I hatched out a plan with an assist from a few key players like Breanne and Cailleach. Maybe Birgit. Arianrhod would be a powerful ally, but she probably wouldn't want to dirty her hands with a problem that didn't impact her one way or the other.

"I spoke with Zottre," I told the council. "I gave him my word I'd describe his plight and the Cait's desire to reestablish themselves in Underhill. He's expecting me to return with an answer."

"What will you tell him?" Breanne arched a white brow.

"That the council declined his request, and he has one week to clear out from beneath Ben Kilbreck. After that, we will force them out."

"It would be far better if the Celts did it for us," Breanne mumbled.

"Not going to happen," I told her flatly. "I sent Hedrek to speak with Arianrhod. She ignored him, which is unusual."

"She's not the only Celt," Kirwan said.

I glanced around the room. "Do any of you have a pet Celt in your back pocket? Someone you can raise fairly soon?"

Suddenly, no one wanted to make eye contact. I'd figured the answer would be no, but this clinched it. "This could be bloodless," I noted. "The Cait might pick up and head for a borderworld. In case they don't, how many of you are willing to field a platoon?"

About half the council raised their hands. Good. It would be sufficient. I removed my palms from the crystal. It quieted, but it had served its purpose: keeping me calm and in control.

"Gather the men and women who fight under your command. Field them and review battle techniques and strategies. Work together. These preparations may not be necessary, but it's not a bad idea to be ready.

"While you're at it," I went on, "take stock of the armory. Make certain no one snuck in here and took any of our weaponry." I'd already checked the council chamber. Nothing was missing from this room.

Breanne lumbered to her feet. "We have grown sloppy," she said in her outdoor voice. "Complacent. Even those of my esteemed companions who do not wish to engage the Cait in battle would be well served to take part in this exercise." Clapping her hands smartly together, she marched out of the room. After a pause, everyone filed after her.

If she weren't so prickly, I'd have hugged her. Good of

her to encourage forward movement—and cut off further arguments about next steps. Why so much sympathy for the Cait? I hadn't expected it, which meant I was out of touch with my people.

I needed to remedy that. And I would after I found Abria.

A quick tour through Underhill revealed she'd been here, and not all that long ago. It was simple enough to track her out of Underhill to the Rait Castle courtyard. Becca had been here too. The unicorn's magical signature was unmistakable.

I assumed they'd be close, but the trail went cold about a kilometer from the castle's ruined gates. Damn. They must have teleported somewhere.

State the obvious, why don't you, an inner voice snarked.

Nothing else for me to do here. At least Becca was with her. No one fucks with unicorns, not if they value their immortal lives. I really didn't want to deal with Zottre again, but there wouldn't be a better time to tell him the council's decision. And outline his choices.

Once I returned, I'd work on my own swordsmanship. A problem with employing magic to fight is the rest of my skills had eroded. From time to time, nothing but a massive broadsword swing would do.

Ben Kilbreck wasn't far. In the space between two breaths, I left the forest near Rait Castle and plopped out half a kilometer from the Cait's current lair. After shrouding myself in wards, I crept forward hoping to eavesdrop on something useful. A prime tidbit I could toss into the council's midst along with an "I told you so."

A fine drizzle dampened my clothes—and my spirits.

Celtic magic zinged this way and that, almost crooning to me. Perhaps the mountain was grateful for my presence. The Cait were so filthy and stinky, nothing forged with clean magic would tolerate them long.

Though I tried, I didn't pick up any conversational threads as I drew nearer. I'd hoped they'd be outside, perhaps sitting around a fire. Not only were there no Cait, not so much as a Leprechaun or Brownie popped up to beg for their home back. I smelled the Cait as I drew nearer. No one patrolled the entrances.

Naught for it but to pop within. A Cait sprawled in front of the entrance I'd chosen, reeking of alcohol and sweat. Irritation zinged through me. I booted him in the ribs. "Get up. Have some respect for yourself."

A groan was followed by two more. "You didn't have to haul off and kick me, mate," he groused.

"Apparently, I did." I nailed him once more. "You will address me as liege. I'm scarcely your 'mate.'"

He pried bleary eyes open to get a good look at me. His mouth gaped, and he lurched upright. "Apologies, my liege." He bowed. "What can I do for you?"

"Better," I grudgingly allowed. "Find Zottre. Bring him to me."

The inebriated Cait shambled down a corridor shouting Zottre's name. What in the unholy hell? Had he lost his telepathic ability?

I rocked from foot to foot, breathing through my mouth to reduce the stench. Even if I were inclined to relent and allow the Cait to return to Underhill, they'd need a crash course in hygiene. No one would tolerate how far they'd fallen.

"You've returned," Zottre called as he ran toward me. When he was about a meter away, he stopped and sank to one knee.

Shock rippled through me. I hadn't expected a show of humility. But it didn't mean anything. Zottre wanted back into the fold badly enough to pretend he was contrite.

"Get up." My voice was gruff.

He did and shrugged. "Worth a try, eh?"

"Am I really that easy a mark?"

Another shrug. "You used to be." He blew out a tight breath. "How long do we have?"

"Before?"

"Fuck you, Elwyn. Don't be coy."

I nailed him with a direct gaze and magic. "I'm not. You still have choices for the Cait."

"Like what?" Bitterness lined his words.

It was a waste of breath, but I had to give this my best shot. The Cait were still Sidhe, and I was their prince. "The reason Earth ejected you from your last home is the way you've sullied her gifts. What happened to taking care of yourselves? To being clean?"

"How do you know about that?" His chiseled mouth twisted into a snarl.

"I was there."

His hands formed fists. "You were behind that. I should have known."

I grabbed one of his wrists. "I said I was there, not that I was the instrument of your downfall. You've done a fine job of that all by yourself."

He wrenched his arm trying to get loose. I held tight.

"I'm not done," I informed him. "You can take the Cait and move to a borderworld. No one will bother you there. If you remain here, either us or the Celts—or both—will march on Ben Kilbreck."

"It's all that woman's fault. The one you were stupid enough to marry."

My free hand itched to slap him. I didn't. "Abria is off limits."

"Fine. Have it your way."

I squeezed his wrist until bones crunched together. Zottre winced but didn't cry out.

"Nay. This is your way. You decided to leave. You decided to engage your kinsmen in battle. You've made a series of ill-conceived decisions that have landed you here."

"If it weren't for Abria, we'd have won that night at Rait Castle."

"I think not. Like I told you. Any discussion of her is off limits." One more squeeze broke at least two of the small bones in his wrist. I let go after that. I'd said what I came to say. No reason to remain. Further conversation would change nothing.

Zottre cradled his wounded wrist. Power flowed from his other hand to repair the damage I'd inflicted.

"There is no way you can win," I told him. "Some of the Sidhe would welcome you back, but the vote went against you."

He lifted his upper lip. "What would you do?"

"If I were you?" At his nod, I said, "I'd leave, let a few hundred years pass, and plead my case once more. We have long memories, but we'd be more inclined to offer clemency if you prove you can coexist with others."

A crafty look stole over his features. I turned and walked away before he embarrassed himself by trying to manipulate me. I was ashamed to be related to the Cait Sidhe. If I remained, it would only deepen the schism. Not that it mattered at this point, but at least one of us could retain our dignity.

"Elwyn," he called after me in wheedling tones laced with compulsion.

I kept on walking. It might be a game for him, but the integrity of the Sidhe was at stake. I refused to sink to his level. To avoid him running after me, I launched a hasty travel spell.

For once, I lacked a destination, but I'd fix it as I went. If I did naught, I'd end up back in Underhill. Surely, Abria would be back by now. The walls of my chamber took shape around me.

I knew at once she wasn't here. Hadn't been since I left.

Not alarmed quite yet, I sprinted for the library. Not there, either. I sent my mind voice through Underhill asking if anyone had seen her.

Silence was followed by a chorus of nos.

Worry chewed a hole in my brain. I couldn't go after her. I had no idea where she was. I'd tried tracking her before I left for Ben Kilbreck, and hit a dead end. Even if I revisited the spot I'd lost her and Becca, I wouldn't find new clues to their whereabouts. After a few transits of the library, I reconstituted my spell and instructed it to take me to Caer Sidi.

Arianrhod might know where Abria was. She could also convene the Celts to do something about Ben Kilbreck's desecration at the hands of the Cait.

She could, but would she? She was far more likely to toss it back into my lap. My people. My problem.

I have a lot of pride, but I'm not above groveling to keep things from spiraling out of control.

Who am I kidding? an inner voice asked dryly. *They already have.*

CHAPTER 11

ABRIA

"Let me tell you a story" hearkens back to almost everyone's childhood except mine. The Celts weren't big on entertaining me. Grateful Becca wasn't shutting me out, I settled onto the ground in a cross-legged sit and waited to hear her tale.

"When dragons left their ancestral home in Fire Mountain and roamed wide," she began, "one of their first stops was Earth. Seeing them streaking across the sky, all fire and light, gave those who ruled humankind ideas."

She settled onto her haunches, forelegs extended so her head was level with mine. Her horn turned iridescent in the muted light of this world. "Men have always been power mad. Some of the early kings got the idea if they could only ride a dragon, they'd rule the world." She brayed laughter.

"The harsh truth was if men even got close to a dragon, they turned into dinner. Not sure what you know about dragons, but they're easily bored. Once they'd mowed through a few hundred humans, they flew off to explore other worlds. Eventually, they returned to Fire Mountain, but the damage was done."

"What damage?"

"Ssht. No questions until I'm done."

I nodded agreement.

"The damage was mankind expecting power to rain from the skies. They went out in all manner of weather, eyes glued to the night sky in hopes the dragons would return. Some were so wonderstruck, they withered and died where they sat.

"During those days, Herne was a mighty hunter in England. He pursued the dragons, as mesmerized by them as everyone else. For some reason, he kept moving when others fell by the wayside. Some said he drew power from a majestic oak tree. Others whispered it was his link with an enormous stag with golden horns.

"The various pantheons issued edicts. Whoever owned the stag was to rein it in. Herne was mortal. He had no business with a magical creature."

My ears perked up. This was a version of the tale I'd never heard before.

"As was common," Becca went on, "arguments ensued. No one claimed the stag. There was a lot of finger pointing. The next time Herne was sighted, he'd attached a rack of antlers to his shoulders and rode astride the stag.

"Danu warned him to leave off. Magic wasn't meant for mortals to meddle in. Herne didn't listen. The next sighting, he and the stag had merged, looking rather like a centaur, except, instead of half-man and half-horse, the new version was half man, half stag. They took to the night sky with an assortment of werewolves and faeries. At first, they were benign enough, but soon they began appearing before natural disasters. Fires. Floods. War. Worse, they scooped the dead into their Hunt, plopping them on horses or goats and riding through the midnight sky.

"Mankind should have feared them. Instead, they built shrines in hopes that they, too, would join the ranks of dead warriors when their time came. Herne and the stag remained one and the same. It was unnatural, an affront to every god, goddess, and pantheon. We tried to catch them, confront them, but Herne was elusive, vanishing at just the right time."

The unicorn arched her neck. Where her horn touched the ground, sparks flew. "What we couldn't accomplish," she went on, "Odin managed for us. He gathered his dead warriors from Valhalla and his Valkyries and formed his own Hunt. For a time, both he and Herne traveled the night skies, but Odin has always had a bloodthirsty side. He sicced his warriors—and his Valkyries—on Herne.

"The result was predictable. Herne vanished from sight —and eventually from memory."

Becca stopped talking.

"May I ask a question now?" I ventured.

She gave me a look as if to inquire what more there was to discuss, but nodded.

"Why the warning to stay away from Herne? If he's who has been invading my dreams, he must need something."

"Don't you see?"

I bit back a frustrated sigh. "If I did, I wouldn't have asked."

"If you befriend Herne, Odin will come after you with all the force of the Nine Worlds. This isn't a battle you can win, and it will put the Sidhe at risk because of your link to Blake."

Duh. I slapped my forehead with a palm. Blake had already had one run-in with Odin. It hadn't ended badly, but there'd been a lot of male posturing. Blake hadn't spilled every detail, but I'd picked up some of what he'd left out from his mind.

"Still, I can't see harm in hearing him out," I murmured. "Listening to him doesn't equate to cooperating with whatever he has in mind."

"You promised." A sharp whinny punctuated her words.

"What I promised was to talk with Blake and include you and other unicorns in any decisions," I reminded her.

"Why would you even want to find Herne? He's a pariah. Goes his own way no matter what others think."

I crinkled my nose, He sounded a lot like me, but I didn't say it out loud.

"Thank you for trusting me with information." I scrambled upright and bowed low.

"You are welcome. Shall we return?" She rolled to her feet and shook out her lush mane.

I vaulted onto her back. By now, Blake was probably turning Underhill and beyond upside down hunting for me. If I'd known I'd be off-world, I'd have left a note. Or floating runes, or something.

Becca and I parted ways in the Rait Castle courtyard.

Our return journey had been quiet. I was considering what to do next. She may have been regretting telling me anything. Before she trotted off, I asked, "Is he still alive?"

"What do you think?" She didn't ask who I meant by he.

"He must be, or he wouldn't be trying to contact me."

"Or it might not be him at all, but one of your enemies manipulating you."

She waved her horn from side to side. "Be very careful, Abria. Do not tamper with energies that could bring all of magic-kind down."

Incurring Odin's wrath was one thing, the fall of magic quite another. Before I could ask what she'd meant, she was gone. Breath whooshed from me. I stared after her and wasted a few minutes wishing for my old life back. The one where I was a mediocre mage with limited power who surrounded herself with animals.

When I'd fixed the problem with the ley lines, I'd assumed magic was safe forevermore. Why did I always end up smack dab in the middle of monumental choices?

Before I got lost feeling too sorry for myself, I went through the gateway into Underhill. It's invisible to mortals and repels them. Blake had set two changelings to guard this entrance. It had cost one his life, and nearly killed the other. Roya escaped, but not before her foster Earth father lopped off her hands.

Rait had been a real castle then, not the pile of rocks that marked its erstwhile location today. Either Underhill was growing more familiar, or it was content to allow me easy access to my chosen destinations. I found my way to Blake's rooms—except I suppose they're mine too now—but he wasn't there.

Runic letters formed in the air in front of my face. They read *fanacht a chur*, Gaelic for stay put.

I mimed a salute, muttered, "Aye, aye, sir," and kicked off my boots before heading for the kitchen. The cold box didn't offer much. Blake had a way of conjuring food, presumably from Underhill's main kitchen. Even though the Faery land appeared to have accepted me, I wasn't certain how to go about ordering a sandwich.

Probably better to go myself.

After tipping half a mead flagon down my throat, I wandered to where I'd left my boots and slid my feet back into them. The spicy, alcoholic beverage burned my mouth, throat, and on down to my stomach, Because the latter was empty, my head took on a pleasant buzz.

I rustled through Blake's desk. Once I located a sheet of vellum, I wrote, "Kitchen or library. Find me when you return."

The words looked a wee bit on the stark side, so I drew a couple of hearts beneath and added a string of Xs and Os before leaving in search of the main kitchen.

After wandering this way and that, I realized I was traveling in circles after I passed the council chamber twice.

Let's be smart about this...

I raised magic and linked with ambient power running through the underground Faery compound. A rough map of Underhill floated before my eyes. All it lacked was a "you are here," sign. But it didn't really need one since the council chamber was delineated, and it was right across the hall from where I stood.

I was studying the floating map, sketching out a route, when Breanne hustled to me. Actually, lumbered would be closer to the mark. "Hunting for something, dearie?"

I smiled. "Yeah. Where are the kitchens? I'm starving."

"But 'tisn't mealtime."

Oh-oh "Does that make a difference?" If it did, I could return to my favorite market in Nairn. They had homemade soup and fresh bread all day every day.

"Not really. If you're willing to make something for yourself."

"Sure. No problem." I didn't bother adding it was how I'd lived most of my life. I'm far from a gifted cook, but I've been producing my own meals forever.

"Kitchen is this way. Come along. I'll show you."

I withdrew the magic powering my map and let it crumble to dust.

"Where have you been?" Her tone was conversational, pleasant. "Blake was looking for you." Suddenly, her words developed an edge.

"Figured he might be. I should have told him I was going, except when I left I didn't expect to be gone long, and I lacked a destination. So, I'm not sure what I could have told him."

"Mmph. Still haven't told me where you were." She gripped my upper arm, impeding further progress. Great. I'd fall on my face from a lack of blood sugar.

"Can we walk and talk at the same time?" I inquired. If

she said no, I was out of here. I'd stick it out in our quarters —or teleport to Nairn.

Breanne took up her slow, inexorable gait with her arm still hooked through mine.

"Blake's not the only one who's hunting you."

Her insinuation was inescapable. "Oh, really. Who else?" I was certain I already knew, but this was one time when I'd have welcomed being wrong.

"Birgit came through. So did a pack of the little people."

I passed a hand over my eyes. Could have been worse. I'd expected Arianrhod or Ceridwen, or the two of them. Probably by now everyone knew I was searching for Herne. The goddesses would take the same tack Becca had and order me to leave well enough alone.

Breanne guided me down one long tunnel after another. Finally, she hip-butted me into the kitchen. "Thanks," I muttered. "I'd never have found this on my own."

"The kitchen isn't fond of being found," she agreed.

I blinked in disbelief. "Why on earth not?"

She shrugged. "'Tis the way of things."

It took me a while to come up with flatbread and cheese. The kitchen consisted of one room with a hearth, a cold box, and a sink. A neighboring room was lined with cupboards and drawers. Worktables ran down its center. Nothing was organized in any cohesive fashion. Because Breanne didn't show any sign of going away, I hoisted myself onto a table and stuffed food into my mouth, chewing and swallowing.

"Where. Were. You?" She inserted spaces in between the words.

Oh yeah. I'd never exactly answered because I wasn't

ready to talk about it. "How about if we wait for Blake to return?" I countered. "Then I can tell both of you. Or the whole council if you'd prefer."

She frowned, her thick brows forming a single line. My guess was no one refused her anything. I kept eating wishing I'd had the foresight to grab a glass of water.

Or more mead.

Power flickered around her. Aw fuck. Was she summoning reinforcements? Did she suppose I had something shady to hide?

Breanne angled her head to one side as if she were listening. When she straightened, she said, "Blake is nearly back. He said for us to wait here for him."

I'll just bet he did.

I buried that thought deep. I was touched he cared about me, but annoyed because I felt smothered. I should have realized becoming his wife would tether me to something well beyond him, but the reality was only now sinking in.

I was licking my fingers to sweep the final crumbs from my plate when Blake strode into the kitchen. Arianrhod was with him. Hedrek flew around them both and settled on the table next to me.

After nodding a greeting at Blake, I waited. Throwing myself into his arms in front of an audience didn't seem the best of ideas.

"Glad you're all right," he said gruffly.

"Why wouldn't I be?" I flapped a hand his way. "Never mind. Didn't mean to sound so surly. I'm sorry I wasn't around earlier. I ran into Becca, and she took me to the unicorns' borderworld."

"Really?" Arianrhod's blonde brows shot up. "I've known such a place existed but never visited. What was it like?"

"Hard to say," I replied. "We only went to one spot, and it was thick forest. I can't tell you where it's located because Becca erased that part of my memory."

"Why there?" Breanne asked.

I glanced her way. Naturally, she hadn't had the good grace to offer Blake or me the privacy of a reunion. "She didn't want to be overheard."

Breath huffed from Breanne. "Why are you making me drag this out of you?" she demanded.

I hopped off the table and faced her bulk. "The short answer is I asked for information about Herne. She reluctantly told me a few choice bits and instructed me to steer far clear."

"Ha. Same thing I told Blake when he wouldn't take no for an answer," Arianrhod chimed in. "Encouraging the unicorns are in agreement."

Things I wanted to say duked it out for ascendency. After a brief internal tussle, I said fuck it and dove in. "Why am I the only one who's curious about why Herne popped into my dreams? Further, isn't anyone else concerned about me riding to war on Becca with Herne by my side?"

Hedrek hooted and rubbed his beak on my thigh. Might have been a vote of confidence. Or a show of sympathy.

"If I ride to war," I continued, "the rest of you will be there too. It will require a modicum of planning, or at least cooperation."

"Not all dreams are true seeings, child," Arianrhod pointed out.

I should have kept my mouth shut, but I rounded on her. "True enough—if it's only one dream, or maybe two. I've had Herne riding shotgun for weeks now. He shows up every night like clockwork. One of these evenings, he'll break through. When it happens, I will talk with him."

Blake crossed to where I stood and placed an arm around my shoulders. "Abria, we believe he discovered your link to the ley lines and is using you to gain revenge on Odin."

"That's funny. Becca is convinced it's not Herne at all but some wicked entity trying to steal my magic. Beyond that, who are you referring to as *we*?" My upper lip curled.

"I spoke with a few Celts," Arianrhod informed me.

"While you were at it, did you float the Leprechaun problem?" I sneered, well past the polite stage.

"Couldn't locate Danu," she replied stiffly.

I shook loose from Blake's arm. "And that's the end of it?" My voice was shrill. "Don't you people ever share tasks? I am not your responsibility. The Leprechauns are. They need you, and badly enough to have come by here hunting for me."

My hands had curled into fists. My breath was coming quicker than it should. Before I totally alienated Arianrhod, I turned and strode from the kitchen. On the way, I cobbled a hasty travel spell together.

It spit me out on Cailleach's beach. I'd no sooner emerged than Hedrek flew through his own portal. I stared at him. "You followed me."

"Aye. You could use someone to listen."

"Pfft. Don't you mean someone to talk sense into me?"

He landed on a flat promontory and gazed at the breakers crashing on Scotland's rocky coast. The day was cold but clear with the sun partially obscured by thick gray clouds.

"I'm not against you," the owl observed.

I plopped down next to him. "Did Arianrhod send you after me?"

"Nay."

Finally, a plus.

"I did," Blake said as he emerged from the same portal the owl had used.

I faced him, hands on my hips. "Spare me the lecture."

He arched a dark brow. "Which one?"

"Any of them." Anger simmered surprisingly close to boiling over. What in the unholy hell was I so spun out about?

Breath huffed between Blake's perfectly straight teeth forming clouds in the damp, chill air. "We need a better system."

"For what?"

"I was concerned about you when I tracked you and ran into a blank wall."

There was no censure in his words, only desolation. It broke through my defenses. I walked to him and wrapped my arms around his body. "I'm sorry. I had no idea I'd end up off-world. Becca agreed to talk with me. I couldn't afford to let the opportunity slip past."

He opened his mouth, probably to ask, "why not." To his

credit, those words never saw the light of day. Instead, he said, "Becca may be right about an entity shadowing you."

I let go and settled my hands on his shoulders. Locking gazes, I nodded. "If it's true, I'll figure it out. I have the ley lines on my side. They're a powerful ally."

His brows formed a tight line. "It's not about trusting you, I do, but I haven't figured out how not to worry."

"I'm still working things out myself," I admitted. "Breanne was furious I didn't pony up exactly what she asked for the moment she requested it."

"No one refuses her anything." A corner of Blake's mouth twitched.

Hedrek hooted and flew a couple of circles around our heads. "What about Herne? And what about the Cait?"

"Is there news?" I asked Blake.

"I stopped by and told them war was bearing down on them."

My mouth fell open. When I recovered, I asked, "Why?"

He shrugged. "To give them an opportunity to do the right thing."

Hedrek hooted. I dissolved in bitter laughter. "Yeah. Like attack us first, or run like hell," I gritted.

"If they left, it would serve everyone's needs." Blake's words were soft.

I let go of him and looked away. A Cait exit would serve Blake well since it got him out from under waging war against his own. But it just kicked the can down the road. Even if the Cait left, they wouldn't stay gone forever. They'd make certain not to return until they were strong enough to mete out significant pain.

The Sidhe were his people, not mine. Far be it from me to tell him how to govern. I didn't think about my next words; they popped out unbidden. After rolling my shoulders back and standing tall, I said, "I don't stick my oar into Sidhe politics. Don't stick yours between me and my dreams."

"They don't all turn into true seeings," he insisted.

"This one will." I closed my teeth over my lower lip until I tasted blood. "Are you in this with me? Or shall I go it alone?"

"Leannan, darling. Of course, I'm in everything with you. Always."

"Then stop fighting whatever this is, and let it play out." Before he could respond, I added, "I promised Becca we'd sit and talk with her about our next moves."

"Good idea," Hedrek hooted.

"Before or after you talk with Herne?" Blake asked.

I narrowed my eyes. Thank the goddess he wasn't going to play the husband card and try to rein me in. He'd have failed, and it would have created a serious rift between us. Blake is highly intuitive and knew to tread lightly.

"Not sure," I replied.

"Fate is in play," Hedrek intoned. "I feel it in every feather."

A chill marched up my spine, its sharp edges prickling unpleasantly. I shivered. More talk felt unwise. "Let's go back. I'm still hungry."

"Sure—" Blake began.

"You returned early." Cailleach's voice preceded her as she emerged from the surf.

Awk. I'd forgotten about our promise to return in two days. Not exactly forgotten, but so much else had intervened, it moved away from center stage.

"We did," I told the witch goddess.

She nodded tersely and tossed wet hair over her shoulders. "Afraid I was unsuccessful locating Danu. I trolled through the Celts, and no one knows where she is. None of them showed the least interest in the Leprechauns and Brownies, either."

"Thanks for trying." Blake bowed in her direction.

"I'm not done. The other issue, the one about Herne. He's definitely alive. Rumor has it he's being held somewhere against his will. It's why you haven't been able to scare him up."

"Wonder where," I murmured.

"Still working on it," Cailleach said. "I'll find you when I know more."

Before I could tell her how much I appreciated her efforts, she vanished in a swirl of blue bits of light. I placed a hand on Blake's arm. "We should head back."

"Of course." Power shimmered around him. The familiar tunnels of Underhill shaped up around us. If Hedrek followed, I didn't see him.

We'd just crossed the lintel into our rooms when Kirwan hustled up and grabbed Blake's arm. "Zottre is here. You must come."

It took a second for the name to connect. So the leader of the Cait was here, huh? Somehow I didn't think it was to surrender. "Careful," I murmured.

"I intend to be." Blake chanted a few words. A fully laden

tray zipped past and settled on one of the tables in the sitting room.

"Thanks for the food—" I began, but he was gone.

Thoughts zinged this way and that, colliding in my head. I told all of them to take a hike and settled in front of the tray. I'd be damned if I'd let indecision and everyone's fucked-up advice ruin my meal.

CHAPTER 12
BLAKE

What in the goddess's name was Zottre doing here? I'd all but ordered him to hightail it to a borderworld. Guess he hadn't cared for my advice. Was he planning to plead his case before the council? Despite what I'd told him, a vote could go either way. Some would be quick to forgive and forget. In their haste to heal the rift, they'd overlook a whole lot.

Don't move ahead of things, an inner voice hissed.

Aye, best to wait and see what Zottre had in mind before getting carried away with what-ifs. I could have quizzed Kirwan but chose not to.

"What did you tell him?" Kirwan asked as we hurried down dirt-floored corridors.

My ears perked up. "What did he say I told him?" I countered.

"That there was no hope of a reconciliation and for the Cait to leave Earth."

Mmph. "How'd he enter Underhill?"

"He stopped at a gateway and requested an audience."

My mouth split in a wry smile. For once, the crafty Cait leader had followed the rules and told the truth. Wise of him in the midst of mages adept at sniffing out lies. It also painted him in a sympathetic light. I didn't have to be in the council chamber to listen to know he was laying it on thick.

The Cait were sorry. They'd seen the error of their ways and wanted to come home. I ground my teeth so hard they were in danger of cracking and then picked up the pace and shot through the double doors leading into the council chamber. Zottre's whining tones reached me before I saw him.

I couldn't smell him, so he'd taken pains to clean up for the occasion. Meant he knew what pigs the Cait had devolved into, and he didn't care.

He'd taken up a position at the head table. Dead center. Actually, he sat in my spot. The nerve of him. But he was trying to prove a point. I'd made it clear the Sidhe would never fall for his line of crap. He was out to sabotage my leadership.

He might not get very far, but this level of audacity was appalling.

I tamped down fury spilling through me and faced him. "Didn't expect to see you so soon," I said, followed by, "Come over here." I pointed at an empty chair off the one side. The one we used for the odd visitor to our halls.

"I'd prefer to remain where I am." He offered a smile with lots of teeth and zero sincerity.

"I'm sure that's true, but you're in my seat, and I'm

about to convene an emergency meeting. You've no doubt come to plead your case before the council. Your allotted place to do so is right here." I patted the back of the seat where I wanted him.

Breanne lumbered next to him. "You heard Elwyn. Move or be moved."

Zottre's gaze took in Breanne's bulk. I could almost see him sharpening his fangs and claws—until she fixed him with a beady stare. I tapped into his mind, a simple proposition since my power trumps his.

He was debating how to hang onto the upper hand. Talk about hubris. He'd never held dominance in my court to begin with. Breanne closed a ham-sized hand around his upper arm and dragged him upright.

He jerked away from her. "Fine. I'll go. If this is how you treat blood, strangers must not fare well in Underhill."

"Most don't," Breanne agreed almost cheerfully. "But then most haven't waged war on us, either." Giving him a push that almost knocked him over, she sent him toward where I wanted him to sit.

Once he'd cleared the dais, I hurried forward, laid my hands on the crystal in front of my usual seat, and summoned the remaining council members while silently thanking Breanne for stating the obvious. The Cait had sealed their destiny when they chose to leave Underhill and wage war against the rest of us.

I saw it like that. So did Breanne and Kirwan. But we were three out of twelve. I made a decision not to drag this out. Once the rest of us straggled in—along with several interested Sidhe who'd heard what was afoot—I raised my arms and shouted, "Silence," to quash conversations that had bloomed around the room.

Zottre, damn his black soul, was treating this like a version of old home week as he greeted everyone merrily. Long-lost friends, one and all. The faux bonhomie made me want to puke and verified my suspicions about his intent. He aimed to worm his way back into Underhill with the rest of the Cait. Once here, they could conquer and destroy from within.

Cats were devious like that, and it was ever so much simpler than waging war from a distant staging point. Nothing would happen for a few years. Enough for my kinsmen to let their guard down.

Breanne stood to my left and elbowed me. I got the picture. Showtime.

After soaking up as much enchantment as I could from the crystal, I glanced up and down the council table. "Thank you for coming on such short notice. You are all aware of our visit to the Cait on their island in the South Pacific. Earth was so disgusted by their slovenly ways she destroyed their caves."

"You can't know that," Zottre protested and jumped to his feet.

"Sit down," I thundered. "Now." One of my other forms, the one where I'm larger and more foreboding, happened all on its own.

Breanne left her seat and headed toward him. Zottre's butt hit the chair fast.

"Better," I said. "After the quake, I went hunting for Roya. The Cait—your people—had imprisoned her deep in

Satan's domain." Turning to stare at Zottre, I tossed a truth net over him. "How does it happen you can send prisoners into Hell?"

The Cait's mouth opened and closed a few times. He was trying like hell to subvert my spell. Good luck with that. He had two choices. He could remain silent or spew the details of his unholy alliance with the devil.

"Cat got your tongue?" Breanne chuckled at her own joke.

Zottre glared at her.

"Abria and I located Roya," I went on smoothly, "but you know what happened afterward. Abria was captured by demonspawn."

"Rightfully so!" On his feet once more, Zottre shouted, "She is who perverted everyone's magic. Her life should have been forfeit long since. She is not Sidhe. You've invited a viper into—"

The next spell I tossed his way paralyzed his tongue. "Abria is daughter to the ley lines," I said, "but all of you know what transpired. She joined with the lines to repair them, and they accepted her as their own.

"Zottre is here," I went on, "to tell you all the reasons we should allow the Cait to return to Underhill. I cannot think of a single argument that wouldn't put the Sidhe at risk. The Cait made their decision when they left. They compounded the problem when they waged war on us. I am calling for a vote. How many on the council wish the Cait to return to Underhill where they can perpetrate harm from under our very noses?"

Zottre banged on the chair. I angled a pointed look his

way. "Oh, of course. You'd like to say a few words in the Caits' defense. You have two minutes, and they start now." I removed the spell stilling his tongue.

After sputtering for a bit, he spread his hands in front of him. "You're mistaken about us, Elwyn. We've seen the light. We were wrong. We beg forgiveness."

I spun one hand in a come-along gesture. "Is that all? Say you're sorry, and all crimes vanish?"

"There weren't that many—" he began.

"You don't require many when two of them are treason and attempted murder," I retorted. "Full-on murder if you count my other changeling. We found his body, but the magic within had fled."

Zottre rolled his eyes. "Why did I think I'd ever get a fair trial?"

I shrugged. "No idea, mate." I turned back to the council. "Calling for a vote. Now."

"Can we ask questions?" Linea asked.

"Not in this case," I told her. "The only thing we are voting on is whether the Cait can return today. We may take this question up again in a hundred years or so. Or we may not. Time will tell if the Cait are truly contrite."

She nodded. "I see."

After sketching a board in the air, I stood back as the council members filed forward marking either yea or nay. After the first four, I breathed easier. This would be a clean sweep.

"The vote has gone against you," I told Zottre after the last vote had been cast. "We will escort you out of Underhill.

You may plead your case again once 100 years and a day have passed."

His face twisted into a snarl. He bowed low, muttered, "Fuck you. I'll find my own way out," and stormed from the chamber.

"Should I go after him?" Breanne asked.

"Nay. Underhill will let us know once he's cleared her boundaries, which will then be sealed to him and all Cait until the requisite time has passed. Thank you all for your time. Is there aught else to discuss since we've come together?"

"There certainly is," Kirwan said. "Are we still going to chase them down and wage war against our own?"

The way he said it told me how distasteful that proposition was for him.

No more need to manipulate outcomes. I looked each council member dead in the eye for a moment before moving to the next. "What is everyone's pleasure?" I asked.

A tide of murmurs swelled, carrying the same sentiment. No one wanted war under pretty much any circumstances. And certainly not against other Sidhe.

Breanne stood and raised her arms. The others fell silent and gazed expectantly at her. "None of us wish to raise arms against anyone," she said, "but Abria has had dreams of riding into battle with Herne and the unicorns."

"Fine," someone called out. "Let her go."

On the face of things, I was sorry Breanne dragged Abria's dreamworld into the light of day, but it might be for the best.

"'Tisn't a matter of letting her go," I spoke up. "In her

vision, she rides at the head of a magical army. I am certain it includes the Sidhe."

Linea got to her feet. It took effort for her to nail me with her silver eyes. She's short for our kind with black hair chopped to shoulder length. When she chooses to let her magic out to play, she's a seer and a damned talented one. Rolling her shoulders back, she stood as tall as she was able.

"I kept quiet when you chose to marry outside the blood—"

Alarm bells chimed, and I held up a hand. "You will not speak ill of my mate. Now or ever."

"You've never silenced us before, Elwyn," she murmured. "Why now? Are you afraid of what I might say?"

Tension radiated down my back and flowed through me into the earth. "Of course, I'm not afraid," I gritted.

"Then hear me out." Without waiting for assent, she continued, "Trouble follows that one. She has magic to burn, enough to twist Underhill into knots, and she's just now coming into her full ability. The Celts knew and did their damnedest to keep her sequestered, but she escaped.

"The world was quiet for centuries—until she met you." Linea shook her head. "It was foretold, that meeting. You couldn't have avoided it if you'd tried, but once met, many paths offered themselves. You chose the one that linked your life to hers. In doing so, you've sealed our fate as well."

"Sealed it how?" Breanne's question had sharp edges.

"Such has not been mine to view, though I've tried often enough."

"If you're going to talk about me, have the courtesy to do

so to my face," Abria called out as she stormed into the room. Power crackled around her.

"This is a council meeting," Linea sputtered.

"So?" Abria arched both russet brows. "Go ahead. Make me leave if you don't want me here."

That wouldn't end well. I did not want a pitched battle between my mate and my people. What was in play? Abria was normally evenhanded, but she'd checked her manners at the door. Or maybe back in our quarters.

"Talk with us," I invited.

"Gladly. Zottre, other Cait, and demonkind are sowing destruction, wrecking everything in their path." She dragged both hands down her cheeks. "Apologies. My temper has never been my best friend. When I heard you talking about me, at first it made no sense, but then I began to understand—"

"Understand what?" Breanne asked pointedly. "Linea is convinced your magic will lead us astray."

"I didn't say that," Linea protested. "My visions haven't been nearly that cut and dried."

The nimbus of flickering lights around Abria's head and torso settled to a soft glow. "I have things to say, but first you must go after Zottre. He's already sicced demonkind on everyone within five kilometers of Rait castle."

Laying my hands on the crystal once again, I sent a summons winging toward our warriors. Six of them filed into the council chamber wearing confused expressions. Wartime hadn't been on the menu for many centuries.

"Find Zottre," I instructed. "Do whatever you must to stop him."

"And then?" Corin asked. White hair was plaited close to his head; a long sword hung from a scabbard by his side. Snug-fitting buff leather trousers and a tunic swathed his tall, spare form.

"Imprison him in the *Dreaming* along with any other Cait you locate nearby."

"Yes, my liege." Corin bowed low.

No one asked what the Cait were doing here. No one questioned me at all. Their group teleport spell spilled light and magic through the council chamber. In another world, another time, another place, I'd have led the charge, but clearing the air between Abria and the council was more important.

"Are you sure you don't want me to join them?" Abria asked softly. "My power could make things easier."

"Aye, but not until we're done here."

"Make it snappy, sister," Breanne gritted. "There's a battle afoot. I haven't missed one in the last millennium."

Abria mimed a salute, muttered, "You got it," and began to talk.

CHAPTER 13
ABRIA

I was finishing my meal when the muted reek of Cait turned my stomach. It took neither magic nor guesswork to figure out who stood on the far side of the door trying this spell and that to break into Blake's quarters. Zottre had tried to clean up, but he'd only scraped off the surface stench.

Did the Cait know I was inside?

Not in a game-playing mood, and sick to death of all Cait Sidhe, I pushed to my feet, crossed the room, and flung the door open. "Looking for someone?" I inquired, followed by, "How'd you get into Underhill?"

Zottre couldn't have faked the shock radiating from him. After falling back two paces, he shook a finger at me. "I rang the bell. How, else? But you. You've ruined everything." Fangs formed, and his human outline took on a glowing aspect as he hovered mid-shift.

I snorted. "Do tell? My recollection is your people

spawned the battle in Rait's courtyard. Tough luck the tide turned against you."

"Because of you," he howled. "You're bad luck."

"Fuck me," I spat back. "The way I see it, I'm not the one who jumped in bed with the devil. If anyone brings bad luck to the Sidhe, it's the Cait. You should be ashamed. Blake is too softhearted."

The fingers pointing at my chest grew claws. "You. Will. Not. Win."

"We'll see who comes out on top."

With a throaty howl, he jumped me, knocking me backward. Stupid, stupid mage. I stabbed him with power, jabbing jolts through both ears. His howls turned to grunts of pain. He tried to rake his claws down my side, but I pushed him off me and flowed to my feet.

Lightning flew from my upraised hands. I was beyond caring if I killed him. He'd caused far too much trouble. I'd almost ended up imprisoned in Hell because of him. Unbidden, enchantment from the ley lines shot through me, starting with the soles of my feet.

I felt myself glowing, changing. Zottre's silver eyes reflected fear. Before I could inflict more damage—or stop him—he vanished. I peered through my third eye, not believing he could have left so quickly. But no trace of the Cait remained, and then I sensed demon residue.

Breath huffed from me. Was it only him? Or had all the Cait signed on with Satan? I sent power winging wide in the world above Underhill. Fires blazed; buildings sagged as timbers cracked. The goddamned Cait were laying waste to the world.

It violated every precept binding us as mages. Humans were never to know about us. Not for certain. Harming mortals was definitely forbidden. Intent on alerting Blake, I stuffed my feet back into the boots I'd discarded. I could have used telepathy, but I figured the council needed to know. Maybe there'd be a coordinated approach, and I aimed to be part of it, not a third wheel languishing in Blake's rooms.

Our rooms, I corrected myself.

For chrissakes, focus on what's important.

Yeah. Yeah.

I tossed a jacket over my shoulders and was on my way out the still-open door when the air began to spin. After the vortex cleared, the stag from my dreams stood in front of me.

Shock vied with apprehension. Breath burned the back of my throat. I fell back five paces and constructed a hasty ward. Safe for the moment, I tested the newly arrived apparition with magic to make certain it wasn't Zottre in one more form.

Nope. The golden stag with his golden antlers was as real as anything magical could be.

I stared up at liquid golden eyes. No point being coy, not after all the dreamtime we'd shared. "You found me. Now, what?"

"You must come with me."

Why is it my destiny to be surrounded by pushy men? I dragged my shoulders back. "Not right now, I'm not. Tell me why it's important."

"Your magic is elemental in what is to come."

I'd heard that line a few times before, and I may have rolled my eyes. "It tells me less than nothing. Look, I'm in a bit of a hurry here."

He lowered his head until I stared at an impressively sharp array of horns. "You're not leaving until you agree. It took me a lot to break through. I might not get another chance, and—"

Yeah, pushy men who can't help themselves when it comes to telling me what to do.

Feeling gutsy, I wrapped a hand around the nearest antler. "Ordering your brand new partner about isn't the way to start any relationship." The horn grew uncomfortably warm. I released it.

"What is?" He pawed at the ground with a hoof, leaving gouges.

"I really am in a rush. Why is everyone telling me to steer clear of you?"

"Odin doesn't want to share the night skies."

Sensing partial truth, I shook my head. "Whatever this is runs deeper than that." An idea took shape. "Come with me. I have to warn the Sidhe council some of their own are running amok. Once that's done, you can plead your case in front of them. If they reconsider—"

"But you have no choice," he growled in his deep, velvety voice.

"Of course, I do. Are you coming?"

Without waiting for an answer, I shut the door, pushed around his bulk, and headed for the council chamber. The clop of hoofs told me he was following, albeit reluctantly. He was in a perfect position to gore me from behind, but I didn't believe he'd do that because he needed my cooperation. He was different than I'd imagined. Less intimidating. As I walked, I thrust about for why.

Suddenly, it hit me. He'd been some kind of prisoner. He said it took forever to break through, and he might not get another chance. Reading between the lines, he was in a precarious position, one that might be jerked out from under him at any moment.

Had I made a mistake prioritizing Zottre over hearing Herne out?

Too late now. I pushed the double doors open and heard one of the Sidhe saying I was trouble, a disruption that would tarnish all of them. Herne slipped to a distant second place, and I stormed into the chamber, disrupting whatever they were doing.

And not feeling the least bit guilty.

Hell if they could trash talk me behind my back. I barked a few insults; I'd have added more, but Blake's stricken expression shook sense into me.

"Talk with us," he invited, trying to smooth things over.

I offered a curt nod. "Gladly. Zottre, other Cait, and demonkind are sowing destruction, wrecking everything in their path. I ran here to warn you." I dragged both hands down my cheeks and took a deep breath. "Apologies. My temper has never been my best friend. When I heard you talking about me, at first it made no sense, but then I began to understand—"

"Understand what?" Breanne asked pointedly. "Linea is convinced your magic will lead us astray."

"I didn't say that," Linea protested. "My visions haven't

been nearly that cut and dried."

I looked from one woman to the other. The one with short, dark hair was Linea. We'd met at my wedding.

"I have opinions," I said, "but first you must go after Zottre. He's already sicced demonkind on everyone within five kilometers of Rait castle."

My epiphany continued unfolding. This had never been about me. The Cait could lay whatever at my feet and label it my fault, but I was a convenient scapegoat. Kind of like I'd been all those years when the ley lines were damaged.

Blake took hold of a large crystal. I figured he was calling someone to do something. Sure enough, six men—warriors from their garb—filed into the council chamber wearing confused expressions. Big surprise. Some of them probably couldn't recall when the Sidhe had last gone to war. Apparently, Herne had warded himself since no one said boo about a giant stag lurking outside the council room doors.

"Find Zottre," Blake instructed. "Do whatever you must to stop him."

"And then?" the lead warrior asked. I searched for a name and came up with Corin.

"Imprison him in the *Dreaming* along with any other Cait you locate nearby."

"Yes, my liege." Corin bowed low.

"Are you sure you don't want me to join them?" I asked. "My power could make things easier."

Presumably, Herne was still in the corridor outside, but he could hash things out with the council without me there. I rather liked the idea of getting a chunk of Cait flesh. They'd been a thorn in my side since the day I met Blake.

"Not until we're done here," Blake answered.

"Make it snappy, sister," Breanne gritted. "There's a battle afoot. I haven't missed one in the last millennium."

I mimed a salute, muttered, "You got it," and considered how to sugarcoat my new acquaintance. Before I could begin, Herne clopped into the room and stood next to me, eying the assembled council members.

Blake loped toward us. Blue-white power flaring from his outstretched hands bounced off the stag.

"What are you doing?" I shouted.

"What are you doing?" he countered. "I forbade you to—"

My temper roared to the forefront. "I'm your wife, not your servant. You do not get to dictate my choices."

His copper skin blotched with color. We'd had some doozies of fights, but none of them in a public arena.

Herne pawed the marble floor making a *skritching* sound that chilled me. "I escaped from Odin's dungeons," he bugled. "If we don't talk now, we may never have another chance before he brings the full weight of the Nine Worlds down on me."

"On us, you mean," Blake said pointedly.

"Only if you wish it," Herne retorted stiffly and swung his antlers from side to side, narrowly missing Sidhe who'd hurried close. He stamped the floor with a hoof. This time sparks flew.

"Did none of you concern yourselves when I vanished?" Another stamp.

"Why would we have?" Blake was back in full Sidhe prince mode.

The stag raised and lowered his shoulders in an approximation of a human shrug. "Why do anything? Why care about anyone outside your immediate family? No one visits the Nine Worlds, not the part where I was."

"Where were you?" I asked.

"Jotunheim, land of the Frost Giants. No one stops by there. They eat anything that gets within spitting distance."

"They didn't eat you," Breanne muttered.

"Because they entertained themselves by draining my magic, allowing it to replenish, and starting over."

Blake spread his wings and moved closer to me. "You say you escaped. After all these years, how did you manage it?"

Annoyance scoured a trail through me. Herne had had more than his share of misfortune. He didn't owe Blake any answers. I've been odd man out most of my existence. It wasn't a comfortable spot. I opened my mouth to tell Herne he didn't have to answer, but before I got the words out, he nodded assent.

"A fair question," he agreed." A better one is how I, who was once mortal, merged with a magical stag."

"Can we hear from the stag?" someone called.

"We are one and the same," Herne replied. "Long ago, a witch drew me a map of how to reach the ley lines. She didn't lie to me. If I was successful, I'd emerge linked with the stag. If I failed, which was far more likely, I'd die in the attempt."

Breath hissed through his lips, making a stuttering noise.

"Obviously, I succeeded," he went on, "but my journey into the depths of magic was how I found Abria. I've known about her since long before Odin snatched me and whisked me to his realm."

Surprise flooded me. How many other mages were aware of my true role with the lines? Hopefully, a small fraternity. It didn't take much of an imagination to envision factions forming, most of whom would view me as a threat to their magical autonomy.

Or a prized pawn to brandish in games to establish power.

"Recently," Herne went on, "something changed. Abria became one with the lines. I sensed her in a way I never had before, and I siphoned more power when the lines grew stronger. The Frost Giants aren't especially bright. They didn't realize anything had changed. It was how I finessed an escape. And why that particular trick won't work again. If they recapture me, they'll make certain I'm locked behind metal so thick no amount of enchantment can drill through."

"I see," Blake murmured and turned his attention on me. "What was the burst of understanding you alluded to earlier?"

He was asking good questions—and so far he hadn't ordered Herne out of Underhill. I twisted until I faced the other Sidhe. "None of the vitriol aimed my way has ever been about me," I told them. "Not when the Celts tried to hang onto me or when I was blamed for magic weakening throughout the world. I've been a scapegoat. Someone to hang everyone else's failings on."

I sucked in a breath and hurried on. "While the Cait—or the Celts—or other mages are busy blaming me, they're using my supposed guilt as a cover to plot mayhem, which they can then blame on me."

"But why?" Breanne asked.

"I'm different. An easy target. Given my pariah status, defending myself was unlikely. Pfft. Given my pariah status, I probably never knew the half of what I was supposedly responsible for."

"We don't have time for this," Herne spoke up. "Odin, or more likely Thor and his minions, could show up any minute."

"Underhill won't let them in," Blake assured him, but Herne didn't look convinced.

"Why did Odin really imprison you?" I asked Herne. "It must run deeper than wanting the Hunt for himself."

"Technically, the Nine Worlds include Earth," Herne replied. "Midgard is the only one where Odin's will doesn't hold sway. He's plotted for eons to alter the status quo. The stag and I conceived the Hunt. It seemed a simple way to offer glory and everlasting life to valiant mortals.

"Odin viewed it as one more segment in a nefarious plot to ensure he'd never achieve dominion over Midgard. It was why he stepped in with his own version of the Wild Hunt and made certain we were sidelined."

I listened closely. What he said made sense, but something was still missing. "Why have I been dreaming about riding to war with you?"

It could be simple, like including me in his plans to vanquish Odin as a hedge to guarantee victory—although I was far from certain I could offer a sure shot at anything.

Or something far more global could be in play.

My thoughts turned toward Zottre. I'd offered to help, but more pressing unfinished business sat in this room.

Herne's head jerked up, ears forward as if he were listening to something.

"I already told you," Blake said, "Odin cannot penetrate this realm."

"It's part of Midgard," Herne argued.

"Nay, it's not," Blake informed him. "Gateways exist from Earth into Underhill, but my domain is separated from Earth by psychic veils."

"You need to answer why you've been in my dreams." I planted myself in front of Herne.

"We are kindred through the lines," Herne replied. "It makes us natural allies."

"Who are we fighting, and why?" I persisted.

"Everyone who's ever wronged us. Your list is far longer than mine. If we strike fast and hard, we will prevail."

"What then?" Blake asked softly. "One of the lessons the Hunt should have taught you is no one remains on top of the heap for long."

"Odin did." Herne rattled his rack.

"He's a god. Most rules don't apply to them," Blake noted.

"Irrelevant. If the lot of you don't take a stand, and do it quickly, you'll be overrun the same way the stag and I were," Herne insisted. "Your Sidhe kin have forged an unholy union with Satan and his ilk. Lesser mages are leaning their way. If you do not act, and soon, you'll end up by yourself with all the rest of magedom ranged against you."

"How do you know this?" Breanne demanded.

"The Frost Giants wile away time with gossip. Because they helped themselves to my power, it offered a gateway into their thoughts. What I gathered alarmed me, so, when the lines' power grew, I borrowed from them to join Abria's dreamscape."

"Why were you convinced I'd help?" I asked.

"Because you have a good heart."

I wanted to smile but didn't. The horned god's confidence in me was heartwarming, but he didn't know me at all. My compassionate side only came up for air every once in a while, usually when I was surrounded by groups of animals.

"Riding to war rarely solves anything permanently," Blake pointed out.

"But if you do not, you may end up imprisoned—or worse," Herne argued.

"I think not," Blake said in flat tones.

"Where do the Nine Worlds factor in?" I asked. If what I'd heard about Odin was true, he wasn't the "ally with anyone" type.

"Holding Midgard separate will weaken Odin, and—"

"Not what I meant," I cut in. "Which side will he fight for?"

"Whichever one benefits him most," Blake replied and made a sour face.

"You can't trust a word that one says," Kirwan spoke up.

"He'll lie, cheat, and connive and then sell out his allies," Breanne agreed.

"Which is why we must do this," Herne insisted.

"Do what, exactly?" I asked.

"Join forces, take our enemies by surprise, and vanquish them."

"You'd get the Hunt back," Blake said slowly. "Advantages for the rest of us are less clear cut."

"You'd establish dominion over the Cait Sidhe," the stag pointed out.

"There are cheaper ways to accomplish it," Breanne said.

Something wasn't quite adding up. The stag hadn't lied, but neither had he come clean about everything. Not even trying for stealth, I crafted a truth net and tossed it over his broad back.

"What did you leave out?"

He tried to shake the net off, but it clung tenaciously. Tough to dislodge magical accoutrements.

Finally, he said, "I will tell you, but we must be alone."

Blake stepped between us. "Anything you have to say to Abria can be said in front of me and the Sidhe council."

"He is close," rattled through my mind.

I glanced around and then felt stupid and searched with my magical senses. Something glinted off to one side, but I couldn't quite make it out. When I deepened my search, the glinty thing was gone so quickly it might have been a product of my hypervigilant imagination.

A jagged gash formed at the far side of the room. Hands pushed the edges wide enough for a person to step through. In full-on defense mode, I sent jolts of destructive power at the gateway. If I had anything to say about it, nothing would pass into the council chamber.

Where in the hell was Underhill? Supposedly, it acted as the master gatekeeper.

"Abria, stop." Blake's words cut into my single-minded concentration.

"But, but—" I sputtered.

"It's one of us."

Of course. Explained why Underhill hadn't cut the knees out from under them. Withdrawing my frontal attack, I hoped I hadn't wounded anyone.

A Sidhe slithered through, battle leathers hanging off him in tattered shreds. Dirt caked his face and long fair hair. "We need reinforcements," he panted. "Demons are pouring out of portals. Many mortals are dead."

"How many Cait?" Blake growled.

"All of them."

I turned to tell Herne this part of his vision had come true, but the place the stag had stood was empty. Blinking, I raced forward, patting the air and finding nothing. When it sank in he wasn't simply warded but actually missing, the fine hairs at the back of my neck leapt to attention.

What manner of sorcery was this? Had Herne left of his own volition? Or had Odin managed to reach through Underhill's protections and grab him.

Behind me, Blake issued orders and called more Sidhe with his magical crystal. Those in the chamber surged toward the door. Blake ran to where I stood. "Where's the stag?"

I shook my head.

"What does that mean?" he pressed.

"I have no idea what happened to Herne," I gritted.

"Not good news, but we can't worry about him now. Do you still want a piece of the action?"

If I'd been looking at myself, I'd have seen green eyes glittering with a thirst for revenge. "You bet I do, let's go."

"Hurry. We must intervene before the tide turns against us."

It appeared it already had, but I kept that thought to myself.

As I ran after Blake's retreating form I reached for Herne with my mind. He was there, but far, far away. *"Where have you gone?"* I projected, but he didn't answer.

Did he need help? Should I go after him? The impulse felt like the right path, the only one. It was so compelling, I drew up short. Blake had enough on his plate without me disappearing.

Underhill's curved walls gave way to nighttime on Earth. We stood in a small forest half a kilometer from Rait Castle. Screams and howls battered my ears. The reek of spilled entrails and blood assaulted my nostrils. Herne formed in my mind: tall, proud, every inch a god.

The summons was clear; I blocked it out. If he wanted me so goddamned much, he could come to me. He'd done it once.

"You're needed here," I informed him.

Three Cait rushed me. I dug deep, channeling power from the lines, and sliced the lead Cait in two. Ha. Hadn't known I could do that. Blood sprayed everywhere, coating me and everything around me.

"Keep it coming," I muttered to the lines through clenched teeth and barreled into the other two.

CHAPTER 14

BLAKE

Something about the whole Herne appearance—and subsequent disappearance—didn't sit quite right, but I hadn't been able to figure it out before one of my warriors resurfaced. The horned god didn't seem to pose an immediate threat, but I didn't trust him. Every instinct I had said he was using Abria. No matter which way I looked at the problem, though, I lacked proof of sordid intentions.

Maybe there weren't any, and my discomfort stemmed from overprotectiveness kicking into high gear. I'd get to the bottom of it later. For the moment, Herne was gone. It freed me up to focus on whipping my people into shape to face whatever the Cait had spawned.

Damn them and their unholy pact with Satan. Usually, the king of Hell would have thumbed his nose at a group like the Cait. They must have promised him something that made him sit up and take notice.

The question was what.

If they'd promised him Underhill on a platter, delivery would be a problem since I hold the keys to Faery. In true cat fashion, they'd have pledged whatever served their ends. When it came time to pay the piper—if it ever did—they'd spew excuses and lies.

And that would be the end of them. Satan's sense of humor was decidedly lacking. While he welched on bargains, he fully expected everyone else to honor them.

Enough musings. Perseverating about unknowns would buy me less than nothing. Battles go better when an army is seasoned, prepared. The other side might be, but we certainly weren't.

To compound matters, Odin was pounding away at the barrier I'd erected to keep him out of my mind. I hadn't heard a peep from him after he'd stalked me all the way to Underhill and made salacious comments about Abria. Had he been lurking on the sidelines just waiting for an opportunity to break through?

Maybe Herne hadn't escaped after all but was part of a shady plan to lure Abria into the open. If they could shanghai her power, victory over virtually any enemy would be a sure thing.

I glanced at Abria. Ordering her to seek refuge deep in Underhill would be her best defense. She'd never agree, and I didn't have time or energy to spare entering an argument I was sure to lose. If I was too heavy-handed, she'd storm off in a huff. Better to keep her where I could see her.

Earlier, when I'd sent half a dozen warriors sallying forth, I'd assumed it would be the end of whatever shit the Cait were stirring up. I'd been wrong. What I should have done was assemble platoons, arm them, and wait to see if they were needed.

For the millionth time, I questioned if I was the best person to lead my people. If not me, though, then who? No one else had ever demonstrated the slightest interest. I didn't blame them. It was a thankless job when things were going well, and a blame game when they weren't.

Oberon and Titania had been gone so long, no one remembered them. Once Oberon formed the council, he'd left for goddess only knows where. He's wily, that one. I'm certain he planned his exit long before executing it. If Titania had second thoughts, they hadn't run deep enough for her to return.

They're never coming back. Pull it together and focus, goddammit.

Breanne positively glowed as she hustled out of the council chamber. Conflict was where she lived. A few other Sidhe wore expectant expressions. Using the crystal, I called out every mage capable of wielding magic and asked Abria if she still wanted to be part of the fight.

"Let's go," she repeated, followed by, "I know you, Blake. You're hoping I sequester myself in a vault somewhere. It's not going to happen."

I didn't bother answering, just slung power about and moved us to what I hoped would be a sheltered location to plan our next moves. Someone had to coordinate our end of things, and we lacked an organized squad structure.

Squelching my inner commentator, I deployed magic to locate my people. Three Cait headed straight for Abria. The same glowing nimbus she'd summoned at will after merging with the ley lines surrounded her. After the first Cait fell, I quit worrying. No Sidhe was a match for her power, and the animals hadn't yet discovered she was here.

Once they did, she'd have an army of her own to command.

The thought had no sooner marched across my mind when rats, racoons, and mice flowed out of the ground toward Abria. Owls, hawks, and ravens flew out of nowhere, circling her head before laying into nearby Cait with their sharp beaks. Wolves, mountain lions, and bears would show up next. Never mind no one had seen a big cat or a bear in northern Scotland for centuries.

If Abria needed them, they'd come. From other worlds if need be.

I wrenched my attention to my linkage with Breanne, Kirwan, and other council members. Each headed up a platoon they'd assembled on the fly. What I needed was an aerial view, so I spread my wings and launched into the air. The forest was thicker than I would have liked. In many places, it obscured my vision of events on the ground.

Demons were a far worse threat than my Cait cousins. They just kept on emerging from holes in the ground. It was how Satan won almost every contest. Sheer numbers wore everyone else down. A few quick calculations weren't reassuring. We might hold our own, but eventually our power would require replenishing.

No matter how many demons fell, Satan could come up with more. I'd often wondered how many of the abominations were scattered through the nine levels of Hell.

Air shifted off to my right. I spun to face Lucifer. Or

maybe it was Beelzebub. I hadn't spent enough time studying Satan's princes to be able to tell them apart. Flame-red hair floated behind him, tangling with black wings. Like most of his ilk, he was naked. He laughed uproariously. Black jolts of lightning crossed the skies aimed at my head and chest.

A hastily constructed ward defeated the first volley. Dipping and weaving to make myself a less conspicuous target, I focused magic of my own at the monster, but he evaded my efforts much as I'd escaped his.

Was he up here to keep me from overseeing the battle? Seemed likely.

Groans, screams, and the stench of blood and spilled guts rose, circling our aerial ballet. After one more useless volley, I whirled and headed for an open spot below. I was done wasting time. We'd finish this.

Because my feet hit the ground first, I held an advantage, one I aimed to hang onto. The second he landed, I pummeled him with lethal blows, forcing them through his shielding once I figured out how to penetrate its weave. Blood flowed from a dozen cut places by the time he opened fire on me. Any illusion of beauty had fled. His chest heaved; fury flared in the depths of his red eyes.

"You're more trouble than you're worth," he growled.

"The feeling is mutual." I aimed for a cheery tone to piss him off. Angry mages made mistakes. So long as he was in a chatty mood, I asked, "What did Zottre pledge for your assistance?"

Lucifer/Beelzebub's mouth split in a salacious grin. "Why the woman. She's the only prize worth fighting for."

In between lobbing jolts of power his way, I laughed like a madman.

"What's so funny, Sidhe?" He sidestepped my latest effort and returned fire. This blast came close enough to singe the tip of one wing. I sent water to limit the damage.

"What? Zottre led you to believe Abria would stand by while the Cait handed her over to you?"

He shrugged and danced around my latest efforts to annihilate him. "Not willingly, but she is merely one. And a woman at that."

"A woman with the full power of the ley lines at her disposal, and every bird, animal, and fish in existence. Cailleach is her ally. Arianrhod and Ceridwen too."

Lucifer/Beelzebub dropped his hands to his sides. "First I've heard any of that." An unpleasant sensation flooded my brain. Somehow he'd sliced through my ward. Before he did more damage, I sealed the place he'd broken my protective circle.

"Find anything interesting?" I sneered. More than ready to end this, I marshaled my resources. He was skilled, but every warrior has weak places.

"You didn't lie," he muttered.

"About Abria? Why would I? What's the percentage in that?"

"To make her a less appealing target." He didn't show any signs of resuming our confrontation.

Should I continue my attack? Since he'd backed down for the moment, I did as well. It was a good time to add information, so I said, "Abria is my mate. I know her as well as anyone.

Both her magic, and what she's capable of." Before he could respond, I tossed out, "She healed the ley lines by merging with them. When I found her, she was trapped within the lines and muscled her way out without alienating them."

I fixed my gaze on Satan's prince. "She is not someone you want to fuck with. She'll feed you your balls on a platter and laugh when they get stuck in your throat."

I expected him to say something or revert to trying to pound me into the dirt. Neither happened. One minute, he was leering at me, the next he was gone. Vanishing mages were becoming a thing. Our little chat must have given him pause. Maybe he was hustling to let Satan know Zottre was naught better than a common liar.

Would I find an unlikely ally? One who'd solve the Cait problem for me? A bloke can dream.

Returning my attention to the ongoing battle, I took to the skies and assessed how things were going. We seemed to be holding our own—for the most part. Abria was surrounded by an animal honor guard. No one could have mowed through their fur and fangs and scales. She picked targets and immobilized them from afar.

Odin had given up his incessant blitz a while back. He wasn't gone—I wouldn't make the mistake of assuming that again—but biding his time. Back on the ground, I moved from group to group offering assistance as I could.

The Cait fought dirty as always—right alongside their demon sidekicks. The dregs of any compassion took a hike, right along with my misplaced desire to somehow reincorporate them into Faery. They'd made their choices—bad ones—and it was too late to rebuild bridges. Not now, and not a hundred years hence, either.

If I'd been more present, maybe I'd have seen the rift developing and intervened, but I wasn't who'd lit a fire under them to go their own way.

Nay, that was their doing.

Responsibility for my people only went so far.

Something barreled into me from behind, driving me facedown into the dirt. I tried to rise but couldn't. The nasty stench of Cait made me want to puke. Fists punched; blades bit through my ward. Warm rivulets of blood trickled down my back and sides.

I channeled power, sending it upward and instructing it to damage whoever had piled on top of me. It would have been simpler if I could see, but my field of vision was limited to the patch of dirt beneath my face.

Dirt.

Still defending myself, I put out a call to Earth. A quake would even the odds. A chasm would be even better, one that sucked the Cait deep into its depths, while leaving me free to rise and fight.

"Only cowards attack from behind," I shouted to cover what I was attempting.

"Seems to be working," someone chortled. Another punch jarred my kidneys, sending pain shooting up my spine.

A familiar hoot told me Hedrek had arrived. Wings swooshed overhead. Grunts from my assailants suggested his beak was finding soft, unprotected places like eyes and ears. Beneath me, the ground began a slow, inexorable roll.

"Thank you," I sent downward.

The weight holding me in place shifted first to one side then to the other. In the center of the next roll, I used a magical assist to stagger to my feet. Blood coated one side. I'd deal with the wound later. Hands extended, I spun in a circle, taking care not to hit a flock of ravens and Hedrek.

No wonder I'd had such a tough time; a dozen Cait were either fleeing or rolling on the unsteady ground as they groaned and sent magic to heal their hurt places. Try as I might, I didn't see a single demon.

Had they retreated?

If so, what did it mean for the long haul?

If it left the Cait on their own, so much the better.

Whipping up magical cords from a combination of air and fire, I bound every Cait stupid enough not to run away. The cords would hold long enough for a quick transport to the dungeons beneath the *Dreaming*.

Hedrek and the band of ravens—presumably Abria's birds—had moved on. I'd thank them later. For now, I hurried to the nearest group with Breanne leading the charge.

"The demons are gone," I told her.

She offered me a grin from dirt-caked lips. "Figured that out on my own," she chortled.

"Catch every Cait you can," I instructed. "Bind them, and send them to the dungeons."

"In the *Dreaming*?"

"Where else?"

Breanne swung a beefy arm wide to encompass nine

Cait struggling against a pulsing enclosure. "Hear that?" she shouted. "You're as good as dead...cousins."

She narrowed her eyes. "You're bleeding. Do something about it."

I funneled a stream of healing water to close the wound. It took two tries since it was deeper than I thought.

Abria ran lightly to me. The herd of animals closed around both of us. "What's next?"

"Immobilize the Cait."

"But over half of them left."

"I'll take what I can get. Come on."

"What are we doing?"

"Wrapping this up with every group of fighters. Making sure they know to ship any captured Cait to the dungeons."

Abria nodded. "I'll take the ones to the right of us."

A burst of white light heralded Becca and several other unicorns. Their hoofs hit the ground, and they cantered to where we stood. The phalanx of animals opened a path before closing around all of us as they made a variety of cooing sounds. Unicorns are sacred—to everyone.

"What'd we miss?" Becca pawed the ground. Sparks flashed where her hoof connected with rocks.

"A lot," Abria replied, "but things are winding down—for now."

The unicorn tossed her head; her horn glowed with an inner blue light. "You're wrong. I and my herd were called here. We dropped everything and came."

"Called by whom?" I asked.

"Arianrhod and Ceridwen."

I glanced around, half expecting the goddesses to pop out of the ether.

"Did they say anything specific?" Abria asked.

"Only that we were needed." Becca looked this way and that. "I smell demonkind but don't sense any."

"They ran off." Breanne joined the conversation.

"Or maybe they're regrouping." Reaching deep, I tested my theory with magic but didn't come up with an answer.

Hedrek floated to land on Abria's shoulders. "Something feels off," he announced.

"To me as well," another unicorn, this one black, spoke up.

Odin picked this moment to resurrect his assault on my mental barriers.

Abria laced her fingers with mine and shared the ley lines' abundance. I kept Odin at bay; the gouge in my side knitted quickly. "Herne is on his way back," she murmured.

I didn't ask how she knew.

On the heels of her words, the stag shimmered into being, vanished, and tried again. Abria sprinted to where he'd appeared and added her power to his efforts.

I had second—and third—thoughts about encouraging him, but perhaps he was a critical element—and the only one missing. Her dream visions had included her, the unicorns, and Herne.

At the head of an army.

When the stag's outline quit wavering, he said, "Our time is here. We must ride."

"Where are we riding to?" I asked, still not trusting him,

especially not with Odin screaming imprecations in the back of my mind.

Herne fixed his golden eyes on me. Staring back was like revisiting the lost ages of time. "Get rid of him," he growled.

"Who?"

"Odin. I sense him within you."

"What?" Abria twisted to shoot me an incredulous glance.

"He's not part of me," I protested. "He's been doing his damnedest to use me as a conduit, though."

"Why didn't you say something sooner?" Breanne snarled and turned toward me, fingers curved into claws. She'd rip him out of me if it was up to her.

I didn't bother to answer. Sometimes the best way out is through. I wasn't making any progress ditching Odin's efforts to ride shotgun, so I dropped my barriers. He practically fell through, landing in a heap on the ground.

Before he could regain his feet and his dignity, I stood over him. "Return to the Nine Worlds. You have no dominion here."

Odin rolled to his knees and thence to standing. He extended an arm toward Herne. "He belongs to me. Release him, and I will go."

I looked from one to the other. So much for my worries about Herne being a shill. The two glared at one another.

"How is he yours?" Becca prodded Odin in the chest with her horn.

The lord of the Nine Worlds took a step back, and then one more. Fascinating. I wouldn't have thought he'd be afraid of anything, but unicorn horns can end even the immortal.

"He is my prisoner."

"No longer," Becca announced. "No crime is worth as many years as you're held him."

Before Odin's possessiveness held sway, I chimed in, "A battle is afoot. Can we count on your Valkyries and warriors—living and dead?"

At least, I'd find out if he'd already chosen a side.

"Battle with whom?" he sputtered.

Herne trotted to stand next to Becca and Odin. "This is what I tried and tried to pound through your thick, Norse skull."

"You impertinent wretch," Odin growled. Power arced from his fingers but bounced off Herne's hide.

Abria glided next to Odin. "Not hearing him out is a mistake—a big one." She nodded Herne's way and crooked two fingers.

The stag shook his antlers. "We ride to salvage magic as we know it. This is bigger than the Nine Worlds. Bigger than your misplaced pride at losing control of Midgard. If we lose, dark power will prevail, and the rest of us will either fall beneath its yoke or be forced off-world."

"You've been buried in Jotunheim. How could you know anything?" Odin demanded.

"Your Frost Giants love to gossip, but they're lazy."

"And a pack of liars," Odin said flatly. "They'd have told me about it."

Herne snorted. "They hate you, just like all your

minions. How could you not know? They've been placing bets about—"

A flurry of whinnies from the unicorns cut him off midstream.

"This prophecy is true-seeing," Becca insisted. "The Celts sent us here in this moment because it was foretold, and we are needed." The unicorn's next words were aimed at Abria. "Onto my back."

"Gather the others," I told Breanne. "We are in this together."

"Where are we going?" She asked the same question I had.

"The nether worlds," Herne answered. "We will wait, but not long. Gather your people."

I turned to Odin. "Are you in or out?"

His usually dour expression lightened. His mouth spread in a grin. "We're in." He shook a fist Herne's way. "I shall return. Do not leave without me and my people."

"You have one hour," the stag informed him.

Power flowed around Odin; when it cleared, he was gone.

"What do you want to do about the Cait?" Breanne asked me.

I considered offering those who wished to fight clemency, but wisdom prevailed. "We have an hour," I told her. "Plenty of time to secure them in the *Dreaming*."

"I'll help," Abria said.

"No need," Breanne replied, her tone as close to kind as I'd ever heard it. "We'll take care of our own."

CHAPTER 15
ABRIA

I walked to Becca. "Do you still wish me to mount?"

She twisted her neck to look at me. "Not until we're ready to leave."

Blake caught up with Breanne. I heard him tell her to send all the Sidhe to this clearing.

"Might I retain one or two warriors to ensure we don't lose any Cait betwixt here and the dungeons?"

A corner of Blake's mouth twitched. I bet Breanne didn't ask permission for much.

"Of course," he replied. "Take as many as you need."

She inclined her head and left, moving faster than I'd thought her capable of.

Zottre was one of the group Breanne had captured. He stood and called out, "Elwyn. We pledge ourselves to you anew. You need warriors. We will fight."

I expected Blake to ignore the Cait. Instead, he switched direction and walked close to the barrier holding the Cait in place. "Why should I believe you?" he asked in a far milder voice than I'd have used.

Zottre shrugged. "We tried. We failed."

"Aye, we've seen the error of our ways," another Cait cried. "Please forgive us."

Blake crossed his arms over his chest. "This pains me, but you have no credibility. If it had been only a single rebellion, maybe. But you've been at war with the rest of us for hundreds of years. You forced one of my changelings from his magical form and nearly murdered another."

"We're very sorry." Zottre hung his head, managing to appear contrite.

"Give us another chance," someone pleaded.

Fucking cats. Nothing but a bunch of manipulative bastards. I started to call them out on their crap, but the Sidhe weren't my problem—not directly. Crossing my fingers and toes Blake's good nature didn't get the best of him, I waited to see what he'd say.

Blake lingered in front of the enclosure,, studying the captives. After a time, he said, "Breanne will be by presently to collect you. If you go quietly and aren't a management problem, I might reconsider the issue of your freedom, but not for a very long time."

"You can't do this." Zottre shook a fist and yelped when it connected with the invisible wall surrounding him and his kin.

"Just did," Blake informed him and turned away.

When he reached me, I said, "It had to be done."

"*Aye, doesn't make it any easier,*" he replied in mind speech.

Sidhe were filtering into the clearing from wherever they'd been stationed. Power blatted against the Cait's impromptu enclosure. When it cleared, they were gone.

Even though my dreams had been a lynchpin, I still knew less than nothing about where we were going, who we'd face, and who our allies would be. Odin talked a good game, but would he show back up?

The bigger question, an inner voice piped up, *is if he'll take orders from Herne, his erstwhile prisoner.*

Herne plodded to Blake and me. "Are all your people here?"

Blake scanned the crowd. "Mostly, except for the few ferrying Cait to the *Dreaming*."

"I can wait," the horned god said.

"Wait for what?" I asked.

"To share what has been shown me about what lies ahead."

"Odin said he'd come back," Blake pointed out.

Herne shook his antlers. "If he's here, fine, but I will not wait for him. That one has delusions he rules the world."

Blake angled his head until he looked up at Herne. "Would you prefer I hadn't included him?"

"He has a role to play. Whether he accepts it remains to be seen."

Talk about cryptic. I hadn't seen anything in my visions to provide clues about who fought on our side. Or exactly who our enemies were. Someone had to lead, though. Or a couple of someones. My furry honor guard nudged me, cheeping and cawing and chittering.

I crouched in their midst. "We will leave soon," I told

them. "But we travel to a place you cannot come."

I readied myself for an onslaught of protests. Hundreds of voices battered me, all demanding to be included.

"I love you all, but this is dangerous. We travel to distant worlds, ones where you couldn't survive. So your sacrifice would be for nothing."

Hedrek chose that moment to light on my shoulders with one talon on each. "I will ensure her safety," he said. "Me and the unicorns."

"Not fair," rose from many throats. "You get to go, and we do not."

"He is magical," I told them.

"Make us magical," a raccoon demanded.

"If I did, I wouldn't have enough magic left to light a candle, much less engage in the battle of my lifetime."

"Blake could help you," a rat tossed out hopefully.

"He would have the same problem," Hedrek hooted.

I wasn't certain of that since he could draw from Faery and Earth, but I couldn't abide the thought of even one brave animal losing its life on my account. I soothed as I could, but it was a losing proposition. Insects crawled into my pockets. Mice too. A couple of squirrels tried to burrow into my jacket.

Familiar enchantment washed over me. My head snapped up in time to see Cailleach, Birgit, Arianrhod, and Ceridwen walk through a portal that glowed brightly. The four women were garbed in snug-fitting battle leathers in various shades. Arianrhod's bow was strapped across her back; a quiver of arrows with golden tips hung from one shoulder.

"Why are you still here?" Ceridwen snapped.

"We were waiting for you," Blake replied. "And for a few Sidhe who had business to attend to."

"And for Odin," I spoke up.

Cailleach shot me a sour look. "Who invited that old geezer?"

"Watch who you're calling old, witch," Odin bellowed. A gash opened in the ether. He marched through followed by at least a hundred warriors. Some were dead, but not many. Valkyries flew after them. Garbed in armor with bare breasts and hair flying behind them, they were beautiful and terrible at the same time. I'd never seen one of Odin's battle-field maidens before.

The leader of the Nine Worlds didn't let any grass grow under his feet. Valkyries were still assembling when he stomped to a position where he could see everyone.

"Form platoons," he bellowed. "Once we have them, we'll draw straws for who leads each one."

Oh-oh. I cast a sidelong glance Blake's way. Were we going to have our very own battle for ascendency before we even got going?

Herne faced off in front of Odin. "You do not get to lead the charge."

"Of course, I do." Odin tossed his gray head and glared from his single eye. His crows, Muninn and Huginn, cawed balefully to assert their master's leadership.

Arianrhod planted herself in front of Odin. "In this instance, I side with Herne. If you cannot give over, you may as well gather up your people and return to Valhalla."

Cailleach joined her. "The reason I said what I did," she

said sweetly, "is because you have a well-deserved reputation for being impossible to work with. Regardless, you do not hold a starring role in what will unfold. Accept it or begone."

"Why do all of you know more than I do?" Odin fumed.

"Probably because you rarely leave Asgard," Cailleach suggested.

"I don't need to. I'm a seer, along with my birds." Odin stood tall. Above his head, Valkyries flew this way and that.

Blake jumped on a nearby boulder. It raised him above crowd level. Using a magical assist to amplify his voice, he shouted, "Hold. We will not do this. There must be unity for us to prevail."

"Unity under me," Odin shouted back.

To my surprise, Blake mimed a bow. "Apologies if I misled you. I did not invite you because we lacked leadership, but for the additional warriors you could bring to bear. Their reputation precedes them, and we welcome your assistance."

Blake eyed Herne. Something passed between them, but I couldn't make it out.

"If you are willing," Blake went on, "we can split responsibilities for our various factions, but we must hold to a unified plan."

"Who decides what it is?" Odin bellowed, still obviously put out by the turn of events.

"I defer to Herne and the Celts—and Abria," Blake told him.

My mouth may have dropped open. I shut it with a snap. Me? He was deferring to me, whose battle experience could fill the first five pages of a thousand page tome.

"And us," Becca neighed.

Seemed like too many cooks, but I kept my mouth shut. As noted, my formal battle knowledge is limited.

Breanne and three other Sidhe chose that moment to materialize. She may be big and boisterous, but she's also sharp as a tack and picked up on the tension flowing around the clearing immediately.

She nodded to Blake. "Mission accomplished. They'll not bother anyone again."

"Thank you," he said.

"What's happening here?" she asked. "I've been to bully-boy fights with less hostility."

Blake jumped down from the boulder and walked to Odin. "Do you accept the terms as offered? More importantly, can you abide by them in the field if someone makes a decision you disagree with?"

If Odin had been a poker player, he'd have lost every hand. No subtlety with that one. His thoughts were visible as they romped through his mind. He'd already lost face when his bid for absolute leadership was shot down. It rankled, but he wanted to claim his spot in magical history badly enough he finally muttered, "Aye, I agree."

Not quite satisfied, Blake snatched a dirk from its sheathe and made a cut in the ball of his own thumb. It took longer than I'd have liked, but Odin finally extended a beefy hand. Blake made an identical cut, and they shared blood to seal the arrangement.

Not that Odin couldn't welch, but this would make it

more difficult. Blood bonds have a way of coming back to bite you if you ignore their terms.

Herne took a position near Blake's boulder and made a loud huffing noise. Side conversations quieted. He speared the Celts with his golden gaze. "Listen while I tell you what I know. Add to my information as you will."

Everyone's attention turned toward the horned god.

"Even before I met the stag, I suspected I was different, that I'd been birthed for a reason far beyond that afforded to most mortal men. Betimes, I believed it true; others, I questioned if my knowledge was aught beyond hubris.

"And then, I laid eyes on the stag. Something within him sang to my soul, called me with a passion I couldn't deny. I tried telling myself it was foolishness, but he crossed my path again and again until the only logical solution was to meet with him.

"When I did, it changed my life forever. We hunted together, raced over the moors together. Through it all, we didn't exchange a word. I knew enough about magical creatures to understand he was no ordinary stag. Not with his size or his golden antlers.

"What I didn't understand was why I was driven to be with him. It was almost like being in love with a woman, one who teased and tantalized but danced away whenever I got too close."

Herne paused. Perhaps he was considering what to say next.

"Wars came and went," he continued. "Plague struck and retreated. Nothing touched me. After a while, I began to believe it was my link with the stag. He wasn't always present, but often enough to satisfy my need to lay eyes on him. By now, he'd allowed me on his back. Never with saddle or bridle, but he took care to keep me safe.

"A year or so after I began riding him," Herne went on, "I caught glimpses of worlds beyond Earth. Or maybe they were part of Earth, but one step removed. At that point, my understanding of enchantments was limited to leaving offerings for household gods or Leprechauns and Brownies.

"Along with those glimpses, I saw a group of dead warriors patrolling the skies to keep people protected from harm. It was how my initial vision of the Hunt began."

He blew out a burbling breath. "Soon thereafter, I saw myself as one with the stag. Two separate streams of consciousness, one body. I will spare you details, but we made it a reality with the grace of the ley lines. Once I had access to power, I saw so much more clearly.

"The army of dead was meant to hold energy in place. Keep Earth clear of evil influences." He rattled his antlers. "Wickedness is nothing new. It's always been here, but my band of soldiers held it at bay.

"Until Odin had other plans."

"Stop right there." Odin pointed a beefy index finger at Herne.

Herne looked down his long snout at the Norse god. "The stag and I examined all sides of the problem," he went on. "What we came up with was you'd been unwittingly seduced by evil. Your Hunt had a completely different impact on psychic energies than ours."

"Certainly, because yours was flawed," Odin grunted.

"Enough," Ceridwen said sternly. "Herne has the floor. You will not interrupt further."

Odin growled what was probably dissent.

"Regardless," Herne said, "this is how we ended up where we are. The important part is what comes next."

Swells of agreement coursed through the clearing.

"In the same way, the Sidhe and Fae attract positive magic, other sorcerers are magnets for the opposite. Satan earmarked specific groups long ago, factions he assumed would fight by his side when the final showdown arrived."

"Who?" Odin bellowed.

I wanted to clap my hands over my ears. Did he even have an inside voice?

"Most witches, sorcerers and sorceresses, trolls, a few rogue dragons... The list is long. Whoever isn't part of us is likely part of them."

"That isn't important. When Abria repaired the ley lines, she launched a countdown. No one could proceed until their magic was at full capacity. And, aye, the other side also draws from our universal well.

"As soon as the lines were whole, the Dark Mage put out a call to arms."

"Who are you referring to?" Odin asked.

"Not Satan. Someone far older, who is steeped in malevolence. I dare not speak his name aloud. It will ignite power to drop him into our midst. This is why evil is ubiquitous. All men—or mages—need do is utter his name, and he shows up ready to wreak havoc."

"If no one knows who he is," I muttered, "it poses a bunch of problems."

"What do you mean?" Herne asked me.

I thought better of ticking the obstacles off on my fingers. Instead, I said, "Apparently, we have to journey to get to those arrayed against us."

"Aye, but they'd have come to us, eventually."

"Always better to take the offensive." Cailleach rubbed her hands together.

"My thoughts, exactly." Herne nodded pleasantly at the Celt.

I racked my memories. Who on earth could he be referring to? Not that I'd spent eons with my nose buried in lore books, but if a universal prototype for evil existed, I hadn't run across it.

"We will travel to a place beyond Satan's domain," Herne went on. "The journey will be long by magical standards and not pleasant. Some of us may not return." He pawed at the rocky ground. "I have been preparing for this moment since the stag and I merged."

Turning, he looked dead at me. "You, too, are a part of this. And the Celts and Cailleach. Beyond that, I do not know."

"The Nine Worlds will be represented." Odin thrust an arm into the air.

"As will Underhill," Blake said quietly.

My lips twitched, but I beat back a smile. Hell would freeze nine times over before he'd let me ride off to goddess-only-knew-where by myself. Even if I weren't involved, he'd still want to be part of whatever was unfolding. Because he was decent, courageous, principled. If magic hung in the balance, the Sidhe would jump in with both feet.

A rush of love so profound it humbled me washed through my body, touching every cell. I made my way to Blake's side, lacing my fingers with his.

"We leave in an hour's time," Herne said. "Make whatever arrangements you will. Meet me at the westerly end of the Rait Castle ruins. Goddess energy is strong there."

"You won't need it. You have us." Arianrhod smirked, and then turned to me, her scrutiny pointed and uncomfortable.

I girded myself to deflect whatever shit she was about to sling my way. I assumed we'd moved past our earlier dissention, but her expression grew more dismayed by the second. Pushing around a unicorn hind end, she marched close. Power engulfed me, prickly and too hot for comfort.

"Stop that," I protested.

Blake tried to insert his body between the goddess and me and ended up on his ass in the dirt.

Arianrhod reeled in her spell or her probe or whatever it had been. "You can't go," she said flatly in Gaelic.

"She must." Herne gave his antlers another shake.

The goddess faced the horned god. "She is with child. 'Tis far too dangerous."

"What?" I sputtered and splayed both hands across my flat stomach. "I can't be." But then, I sent magic of my own deep within and was met with the beat of a heart. More a flutter, but life—female life—was taking root within me.

I reached deep, wanting to coo and nurture and assure the embryo I'd love and cherish her until the end of both our days. It would have to wait. For now, I sent love and comfort. We'd have forever to get to know one another.

Blake was back on his feet. His hands crisscrossed over mine as he did his own assessment. Before I could tell him I was sorry, that I'd truly been careful, his eyes lit with joy, and he swept me into a tight hug babbling in Gaelic so old I barely caught one word in five.

Cailleach and Ceridwen crowded close. Birgit too, with Jethro by her side.

"The babe will be a queen," Ceridwen announced. "For I have seen such in my cauldron."

"First, she must be born," Cailleach muttered sourly.

"Of course, she'll be born," I sputtered. "I'm immortal."

"Some things are treacherous even to those with unlimited lifespans," Becca reminded me. Her horn gleamed in sunlight streaming through the forest. It could end anyone, immortal or not.

The unicorns formed a protective circle around us all. More than anything, they gave me hope. With them meting out death, we had to win against whatever fortune tossed our way.

"We leave in an hour," Herne repeated. "Whoever is at the appointed spot will come with us."

The familiar scents of Blake's magic—damp stone and rain-wet forest—surrounded me. The clearing fell away replaced by the walls of our home in Underhill. His spell had barely cleared when he said, "We must talk."

Oh-oh. Was he going to order me to remain behind? That wouldn't go well. All it meant was I'd be forced to track the group's trail.

Wait, a wise inner voice counseled, *until you see what he has to say.*

CHAPTER 16

BLAKE

Abria was pregnant! I couldn't stop smiling, and I was damned if I knew why. I've never hankered after children. Most of us don't have any. When you live forever, if even a small percentage of us reproduced, Underhill would become far too crowded.

From Ceridwen's comment and my own assessment, the child would be a girl. I promised the universe she'd have everything she wanted from the moment she was born. When I laid my hands across Abria's belly and felt life within, protectiveness seared me. I'd call out every resource at my disposal to ensure the child not only survived but thrived.

The living room of my apartment took shape around us. I disentangled my arms and placed my hands on Abria's shoulders. We had little time and needed to face this squarely. No time to pussyfoot around the issue.

"Surely, you aren't still considering coming along," I

said. "We have adequate firepower with the Celts and the unicorns and Herne."

A mulish look crept across Abria's lovely features. She shook free of my hands and placed hers on her hips. "It's quite simple. You can leave without me, but if you do, I'll employ every scrap of magic at my disposal—including the ley lines—to follow you. While I'm doing so, I'll be far more vulnerable than if I'd gone with you in the first place."

"This isn't about you." I softened my words as much as I could manage.

She rolled back on the balls of her feet and skewered me with her green gaze. "It's about all of us. About ensuring we can access our power forevermore. If we lose this battle, and we might, what kind of world will we provide for our daughter?"

"Be reasonable," I pleaded.

"I am being reasonable. I'm pregnant, not sick or disabled." She stabbed the air with a forefinger. "You need my magic. I'm daughter to the ley lines. They respond to my need even without a direct summons from me."

"We can do this without you," I insisted, feeling desperate.

She shrugged. "Fine. I'll be there one way or another." And then she narrowed her eyes. "Do. Not. Discount. My. Power. Not now. Not ever. Whatever vision Herne had included me. I am elemental to what is about to unfold, and I will be there goddammit, no matter how many ways you order me to stay home."

"I couldn't stand it if something happened to you." The words tore out of me.

A goddess carved from marble couldn't have looked more noble when she said, "I feel the same way about you." Walking close, she laid a hand on my arm. "We're stronger together, Blake."

I shouldn't have, but I folded. I put my arms around her and just held her against me. When she turned her face up, I crushed my mouth over hers, tasting her sweetness.

Passion, lust, need, blindsided me. She grabbed handfuls of my shirt, twisting the fabric as she sparred with my tongue. I bit her lips; she raked nails across my neck. Between us, my cock swelled to fullness. The hand that raised welts of heat across my skin jammed against my belly jockeying the laces of my trousers aside.

My chest was tight; breathing came in big gulps. The timing was bad, inconvenient. I should be going over a checklist of last-minute items to ensure my people had what they needed, but they were all long past grown. They didn't need Daddy to remind them to take potions, powders, or crystals if they used them. Or to stop by the armory for weapons.

With our mouths still glued together, I joined the fight for space between our bodies and undid the snap and zipper holding her britches in place. Pushing away from me, Abria sank to her knees and took me in her mouth, licking, sucking, nibbling as she ran her tongue up one side of my shaft and down the other.

Sensation cascaded through me, sharp, urgent, intense.

I reached for the vee between her legs but couldn't quite reach it. She moaned and writhed as she worked my cock between her hands and mouth.

"Hold up." I could barely get the words out. Dropping to the floor, I shoved her trousers down to mid-thigh level and dipped my fingers into the streaming core of her.

Somehow we ended up on our sides with my cock in her mouth and my tongue scribing circles around her clit. We've had plenty of practice with semipublic sex. The specter of discovery always adds an edge to our pleasure. This wasn't any different. Sidhe warriors could drop in at any moment as they prepared for war.

Hovering between guilt and need, I sucked hard on her nub. She dissolved around me. It was more than enough to release my own flood. I came for long, intense moments.

And then I came to my senses.

After a final nuzzle of her sex, I pulled away. She let go too.

"We shouldn't have done that," she murmured, "but five minutes one way or the other can't harm much."

"Never could resist you." Twisting around, I kissed her, tasting my jism on her mouth. My errant appendage begged for more.

"The feeling is mutual." She pulled up her trousers and grinned in a wanton way that always hit me dead in the crotch. "I assume this means you've moved past ordering me to the scullery to wait out the war."

The question sobered me. "I'd still rather you remained in Underhill, but I won't toss roadblocks in your way."

"Good choice." Kissing me lightly, she got to her feet and headed for the kitchen.

After setting myself to rights, I joined her.

"Hungry?" She pointed at a plate of crackers and cheese she'd set on the small table.

"Always. You figured out how to conjure food from the kitchen, I see."

Abria nodded. "It wasn't hard."

After pouring a couple of tumblers of mild mead, she joined me at the table. "Any idea how long we'll be gone?" she asked.

"Not really. Magical wars never last long, though." I stopped. "What I mean is an actual war can last centuries, but the parts where people are fighting tend to be quick."

"Mmph." She put cheese on a cracker and popped it into her mouth. When she was done chewing and swallowing, she said, "Too bad we didn't have someone scry this so we'd be better prepared. I also wonder where Herne vanished to. He didn't seem to have any trouble returning at an opportune time."

Her words caught me by surprise. "You don't trust him, either?"

"Not entirely. How could I? It seems he's doling out information on a need-to-know basis."

"We'll find out soon enough." I shrugged. "We'll have plenty of assistance if his intentions are less than altruistic. Besides, I admit I'm curious who this dark mage is."

Her eyes widened. "You don't know, either?"

"Nay, and I spent a chunk of my youth with my nose buried in lore books."

My front door opened and closed. Kirwan strode into the kitchen and took a slice of cheese. "We're ready," he announced. "The others sent me to find you."

I drained my mead. "We're ready too."

Kirwan eyed Abria. "And what did the lass decide?"

"I'm right here," she said acidly. "The lass decided to tag along. Both of us." She patted her stomach.

"Congratulations!" Kirwan's wrinkled face was wreathed in a smile. "We're all excited about Elwyn's heir."

Hoping Abria wouldn't take offense and say the child was her heir too, I rose. "Do we need anything we don't already have?"

"Nope." She crinkled her nose my way. "The animals all want to come along, but this isn't a journey they'd survive. The sooner we're gone, the better. It will discourage my entourage from trying to join us."

We walked out of my rooms. I warded them behind us. Rather than teleporting, we walked to the stairs leading to Rait's courtyard. May as well conserve magic where we could.

I heard the crowd before I saw them. Sidhe and inhabitants of the Nine Worlds stretched so far across the green I couldn't see everybody. How were all of us going to manage? We were too many for a single teleport spell.

Herne must have come to the same conclusion. He trotted to my position at the head of the Sidhe; a series of images spilled through my mind. Not a single journey spell, but three. Once I'd received them, he moved to Odin and presumably did the same thing.

"Abria comes with me," Becca announced as she clomped close.

I hadn't anticipated that development, but I should have

since it was a key element in Abria's visions. I almost requested a unicorn of my own to ride so I could join them, but my duties lay with my people. I had to lead them into battle, something I'd be unable to do if I joined Abria and Becca.

"It will be all right," Abria assured me and leapt onto the unicorn's back.

Birgit glided over with Jethro in her arms. After a quiet conversation, she mounted a unicorn as well.

Cailleach joined Herne, Abria, Birgit, Jethro, and the unicorns.

Ceridwen joined Odin and his army.

Flickers and flares reminiscent of a thousand suns seared my corneas. When they cleared, Herne was gone. Abria and the unicorns too.

Arianrhod ran lightly to my side. "We worked this out while we were waiting," she explained. "Herne and his cohort travels first. After a quarter hour, we follow, and then Odin and his people."

"The enemy won't wait until we're fully arrayed," I noted.

"We know, but it can't be helped. The energy channels allowing us to teleport cannot handle such a mass at one time."

I rocked back and forth on the balls of my feet. Worry for Abria ate at me. She'd be there for precious minutes before I arrived, and—

My task is to lead my people, I reminded myself. What on earth had I been thinking? That I'd drop everything to locate Abria.

"It's time," Arianrhod announced. "You and I will control the casting."

A bolt of incalculable power hit me in the solar plexus. Fighting against it was pointless, so I opened myself to her talent. Between us, a visible net blossomed. Once it was fully grown, it draped around all the Sidhe. I ran a quick check to make certain we hadn't left anyone out.

"Ready," I told Arianrhod.

"No one is ever ready for what we face," she said so softly I may have been the only one who heard her.

"Tell me what you know."

"No time and no point. You'll be in the thick of things soon enough."

All I provided was magic. She managed everything else. I did examine the checkpoints Herne had given me, though. The Celtic goddess was reading from the same script. At the two-thirds mark, she said, "Next stop we'll be in the midst of everything. Tell your people to ward themselves as best they can."

I sent word up and down our lines and was met with grumbles. Fighting warded is restrictive on so many fronts.

A sudden chill of premonition waltzed down my spine leaving ice chips in its wake. The rest of today would alter magical history for eons to come. I girded myself, ready for whatever Dame Fortune threw our way.

I tried for reassuring, but my inner senses weren't buying it. Regardless of whether Herne was walking us into a trap, hard fighting lay ahead. Some Sidhe would never return to other than the *Dreaming*. Others might be maimed.

We'd do the best we could. While not born warriors like Odin's crew, we manage to hold our own.

"Soon," Arianrhod muttered. Still more power streamed from her.

I felt resistance. Something didn't want us breaking through the barrier between us and where Herne was.

For long moments, the push and pull of psychic energies buffeted me this way and that. Finally, I braided some of my magic in with the goddess's. It did the trick. We broke through into no-man's land.

A desolate landscape littered with dead vegetation spread around us. Above, the sky was gunmetal colored and hosted a single, orange sun. From the sound of things, the battle was to the west off to our right.

We waited, Arianrhod and I, until all the Sidhe were accounted for.

She stood at the head of the assemblage. "Strengthen your warding," she instructed, "and then follow me."

"Who's in charge?" Breanne yelled. She's all about military structure, so the question was important to her."

"Elwyn and I," Arianrhod replied. "But most of your decisions today will be independent. Make the best of things, no matter how desperate your situation."

On that cheery note, she headed toward the west. I paced next to her grateful for her abundant power. After half a kilometer, it felt as if we were slogging through demon-tainted slime. I couldn't see it, but I sensed it all around me dragging at me, urging me to leave off and go home. The stench of decay filled my nostrils and twisted my stomach into a hard knot.

Insidious whispers battered me, told me our quest was hopeless.

"Don't listen to the voices." Arianrhod's tone was sharp.

Good advice. I borrowed a stream of her power to plug my ears. It helped some.

A crack opened in front of us, splitting the hard-baked dirt into two sections. Arianrhod stopped, studying this new development. "We go left," she muttered.

"How can you know?" Damn it. Hadn't meant to say that out loud. "Never mind," I added.

"Trust your allies," she said acidly. "The way the others win is by dividing and conquering."

"Got it."

More cracks formed, almost as if they were herding us. We jumped over a few to maintain our direction. Baying and screeching nearly deafened me. A pack of monsters with wolf bodies and raptor heads charged.

Relieved to be doing something other than picking our way through an inhospitable plain, I sent power at the nearest creature. It exploded in a ball of stinking protoplasm. If I hadn't ducked and lunged, it would have hit me square in the chest. When I turned to make certain where it ended up, the thing had begun to remake itself. I sent another volley. And another, mixing magics to up my odds of success.

No matter what I did, the bastard picked himself up and began repairing the damage. Shit. If we couldn't kill or immobilize them, this would be the longest magical war in recorded time.

"Stop thinking." Arianrhod danced past. "Fight. Some of their bravado is illusion."

"Good to know." After sprinting to my latest victim, I prodded the burning ball he'd turned into. It fell apart like so much faery dust—and didn't come back from the dead.

I fell into a rhythm. If I didn't totally kill some of the enemy, I could live with it. We had to make it through this pack of whatever they were to find Abria and the unicorns. I hadn't seen hide nor hair of the Norse contingent, either.

I was bent over a dissolving wolf when something pierced my warding and jabbed into my back, boring through my body. Pain clawed at me. I jammed my jaws together so I wouldn't scream in agony.

When I glanced down, a spear went all the way through me. Blood spewed from the stomach side. Fuck. I could fix this, but I needed time. Whoever gored me had moved on. Staggering off to one side, I chopped off the front of the spear with flagging magic. Reaching behind me, I pulled the rest of the horrible weapon out of my body and send rivers of healing magic to close the wound.

Dizzy. Couldn't get my bearings, but at least the bleeding had stopped. I slid to my knees, but even that was too hard. On my belly in the dirt, I breathed easier. I'd just shut my eyes for a moment. Take a small break, and—

"Oh no, you don't," Arianrhod shrieked next to my ears. "Up with you, or the poison will do its dirty work."

"What poison?" I managed before everything went black.

CHAPTER 17

ABRIA

Herne hadn't been kidding when he said the journey would take a while, even by magical standards. Cailleach straddled the stag. I was on Becca. Birgit and Jethro sat astride a black unicorn. The others stood nearby, horns gleaming with anticipation.

After a while—time is tough to judge in travel channels—Cailleach leaned forward. "Sure you know where you're going?" she murmured. Her voice was pitched low, but because I was paying attention I caught her query.

Herne made a snorting sound, followed by, "Soon."

Cailleach might be in a hurry, but I clung to these last few moments of relative normalcy. They might be the last I'd ever know. Coming face to face with evil changes a person. I'd felt shifts in my inner landscape after my last brush with demonkind where they'd chucked me into an iron cage.

No one told them metal doesn't impact my magic, and

the lapse had worked in my favor. Whoever we faced this go round probably wouldn't make rookie mistakes like that. A shiver trickled down my spine; I laid both hands on Becca's neck, taking comfort from her solid warmth beneath me.

"Are you ready for this?" she asked quietly.

"Not really, but it's going to happen anyway."

"We don't have a choice," the unicorn noted, and then added, *"Glad I was wrong about Herne."*

I nodded. She couldn't see me, but she'd get the drift.

Subtle shifts in Herne's casting alerted me our elusive destination was nearly upon us.

His words clinched it. "Ready yourselves. We won't have much time between when we arrive and when we're visible to whoever is on the other side."

Warding not of my own making clunked around me. Becca's work, and not something she'd have done before. The unborn babe shifted everyone's equation. It should impact mine, but the reality hadn't sunk in. Not quite yet.

I laid a hand over my belly. Once this was over, I'd figure things out. Motherhood had never been even a distant blip on my radar. I could have hoped for different timing... Honesty intruded, kicked me in the shins, and reminded me whoever was running the show had chosen the timing of a new magical being's appearance.

I refocused before my control freak genes had a meltdown.

Discordant noise battered me; pain ratcheted through my head. The infinite black of our travel channel burst outward. Booming, screeching, grinding escalated. Heat seared me. Hotter than a hundred suns beating down, it sucked moisture from my body.

I twisted this way and that trying to see something, anything, but it was like peering through a bowl of gelatin. Since my earth eyes weren't cooperating, I switched to my third eye, and wished I hadn't.

A scene from the worst grade B horror flick ever spread before me. A wasted world in grays stretched to all sides marked by huge rents in the ground and even larger boulders. Macabre creatures that looked like a genetic experiment gone wrong dripped saliva from wicked-looking fangs. Pterodactyl-looking birds perched on the boulders. Long, red talons scratched runnels in the stone.

Two types of monsters squatted in the dirt. One looked like a cross between a wolf and a bird of prey. The other was larger, like a wooly mastodon with a boar's head. For all their fanfare and noise, something held them back.

I braced myself to meet whoever was running this show.

Evil was everywhere. A smell, a foreboding sense bearing down on me. Grit swirled through the air, burning my nose and making my eyes feel dry and scratchy. I clutched at my link to the ley lines. If ever I needed strong magic, it would be soon. At first, I couldn't find them, but then they flickered to half a life.

Something about this place muted everything not aligned with darkness.

I focused on Becca's warmth beneath me, on her steadiness, on the glow of her horn. Beacon against the darkness, its gleam provided a raw of hope.

"We need to do something," I murmured.

"Not yet," she replied.

"Steady," Birgit counseled from next to us.

I started to ask what we were waiting for but didn't. Cailleach and Herne hadn't made any moves yet, either. Was everyone mesmerized by the same creeping evil that had me in its gunsights? If we waited too long, would we lose the ability to do anything but sit here until someone sicced the genetic experiments gone wrong on us?

The obscene noise escalated. Before my eardrums burst, I piled magical protections over them. One of the bird-things launched from its perch flying straight toward us. Becca waited until the last possible moment and speared it neatly with her horn.

As if its dying squawk had been some kind of call-to-arms, the rest of them flew at us. The sharp stench of poison warned me their saliva was toxic. Before we could regroup, the ground animals attacked too.

Becca's ward took twice as much power to shoot through. I jumped down, shucked it aside, and pushed what should have been lethal blows through my fingertips. My first efforts were wasted. They bounced off scaled hides. All around me, unicorns gored whatever got close. Anything arrayed against us needed to be dead.

I changed things up. Added water, but it seemed to energize the monsters. Finally, when my mixture was three parts fire, one part air, I gained traction and became more than dead weight.

A mastodon charged. My efforts weren't even slowing it down. I dug deep, pulled heavily from the ley lines, and stood my ground. The thing bore down on me with its hideous mouth wide open. The stench was unbearable. Worse than every rotten thing in the universe combined, with overtones of poison just like the birds.

"Die, you fucker," I screeched and gave it everything I had.

It kept coming. Becca had become separated from me. Each unicorn was surrounded by a seemingly endless army of monsters. Where were they coming from? However many I'd counted at the beginning had swelled by a factor of ten.

Herne sat in the midst of his own circle of Hell, and I couldn't locate Cailleach. What was wrong with me? Why was my attention wandering? I slapped protections around my mind and homed in on my personal mastodon. Only a couple of meters separated us.

Ha! Proximity had to be the key. The closer it got, the better my odds. I've never been shy on guts. Maybe on brains, but never on grit.

"Come on." I altered my tactic from curses to honey. "Come to Mama."

My last series of bolts connected. The thing crumpled and fell just before its jaws would have closed around my upper arm. Somehow I'd known I had to let it get this close before even my renovated formula had an impact.

"Bravo!" Birgit shouted and killed another just like it. I couldn't see Jethro. He must still be in his cat form. He could do a lot of damage since he was so small no one noticed him until it was too late.

The monster twitched in death throes. I sidestepped my way around it not worried about finding my next target. It would find me soon enough, but we needed a better strategy. We'd eventually run out of juice. Even the unicorns couldn't go on forever without rest and nourishment.

Herne had apparently come to the same conclusion.

"Show yourself," he bellowed.

"Hold!" I shouted. "Where are the others? We all went to the same place." The second the words were out, a slice of clarity speared the murk that had had me in thrall since our arrival. Not that I could think clearly, but at least I understood I wasn't playing with a full deck.

Colors cascaded down a rock wall to my right. It vanished. Odin, Thor, and a group of bloody Valkyries came into view. Hel slithered into my field of vision flanked by her serpents. I'd never met her, but I'd have known her anywhere from the description of how half her body was nothing but bones.

Unaware of us, they were slugging it out with a different set of monsters.

Cailleach twirled in front of me shouting, "It was illusion," as she headed for the far side of the wasted landscape.

It might have been her words, but Odin spun and stared right at me. I have to hand it to him, he didn't waste time with questions, just bellowed at his minions to join forces with the rest of us.

If they'd been within a stone's throw all along, it must mean Blake and Arianrhod and the Sidhe were equally close. I didn't realize till then how worried I'd been about them. My mind had been so muddled, so not my own, any forward movement had taken a ridiculous amount of effort.

I'd lost myself in fighting, but even then I hadn't been

especially effective at anything beyond keeping myself upright.

Whoops from Cailleach—I'd recognize her voice anywhere—alerted me another barrier had fallen. I shot a nearby pterodactyl out of the sky and sprinted toward where I'd heard her yell.

Sure enough, a whole other field of battle stretched to infinity. With the same scorched earth motif as the rest of this goddess-forsaken shithole, this portion contained Sidhe. Arianrhod was yelling, exhorting someone to get up before poison overcame them.

Crap. Who would be stupid enough to inhale the toxic crap oozing from all these misshapen beasts? Arianrhod seemed to have the matter well in hand, but something wasn't adding up.

If the Sidhe were here, Blake had to be somewhere. Why wasn't he tending to his fallen kinsmen? Or why hadn't he called in a Sidhe healer? From my brief tenure with Arianrhod, her nursing skills left a lot to be desired. She possessed talent in spades, but scored zero in the compassion department.

Forgetting her for the moment—healing has never been my strong suit—I focused on locating Blake.

I tried to ignite my link to him, but it balked, backfired, and then guttered and died. Must be my power malfunctioning much as it had since we arrived. Maybe not exactly malfunctioning, but not working quite right, either. Shadows intruded, muddying my mind, whispering insidious suggestions about walking into outstretched jaws with my jugular primed for feeding.

What the unholy fuck? I shook myself hard. Were vampires mixed up in this somehow? They're old but far from ancient. Legends I was familiar with pegged their ascension to Medieval times. Whatever lurked behind this mess had its roots in the beginnings of all worlds, and—

"Abria!"

Arianrhod's shout shattered my worthless musings and brought me at a dead run. Far more than my name rang through the desperation in that one word. I wasn't watching where I was going, tripped over a pile of rocks, and banged my shins on the way down. Undeterred by agony shrieking up both legs, I employed a magical assist back to my feet and kept on running.

It took forever to claw my way past what was left of the barrier that had separated our part of the chamber from all the rest. Jagged places caught my flesh, and the smell of my own blood spurred me to slather magic over every gash. Blood holds power. I couldn't afford to donate any of mine. Things were tough enough. If one of those twisted monsters got so much as a drop of my essence, they could immobilize me.

Or worse.

Finally, I spied the goddess like a blonde sentinel with her arms around Blake holding him upright.

Awk. Christ. Was he why she'd been yammering on about poison? My heart skipped several beats. Fear thrummed a tattoo down my spine.

The battle raged around me. I ignored it, my eyes and heart focused solely on the man I loved, the man who meant everything to me. It took forever, as if I were moving through sticky molasses, but I reached them and wrapped my arms around Blake from the side.

"Blake!"

When he didn't respond, I tried again and shouted his name directly into his magical center. Life thrummed through him, but his mind was far away. Too distant for me to reach him even with telepathy.

Arianrhod is never chatty, but she'd been grim-lipped and silent since my arrival.

"What happened?" I asked.

"Poison spear." She pointed at a bloody shaft stuck into the ground. "I healed the wound and neutralized all the blood drippings, but the damage runs far deeper."

"Can you counteract the toxin?" I demanded. She was the virgin huntress for chrissakes. Meant she could do damned near anything.

"Don't you think I've been trying? Be careful the darkness doesn't suck you into its maw."

"I'll do what's needed," I said stiffly. I had to reach wherever Blake was trapped. If it tossed me into the path of a speeding train, so be it.

She was still holding him upright. I changed position and gripped both sides of his face. No wonder the goddess hadn't had much luck. Wickedness lashed out through my fingertips threatening to snag me too.

"Good luck with that," I muttered and planted both feet. I called on the ley lines, let them flow through me and on into Blake. His face contorted in agony.

"Do not let them win," I gritted and held on. I'd stay the course or die in the effort.

Nothing was working. Desperate, I merged with the lines exactly as I'd done when I healed them. Once I was confident of our combined power, I joined my consciousness with Blake's.

Holy godhead!

He stood alone on a flat patch of pockmarked blood-red dirt. An army was arrayed against him led by a cowled figure garbed in filthy, tattered black robes. The only visible part of his (her?) face was glowing red eyes. No wonder Blake had been unreachable. He was conducting a battle, one he had no chance of winning.

Not by himself, but overwhelmingly negative odds hadn't stopped him.

"I'm here now," I told him. "Me and the lines."

If he heard me, he didn't give any indication, just kept charging, slashing with a golden sword set with flashing gemstones, withdrawing, and doing it again. Sweat ran down his dirty face; fire flared from his eyes.

He wore a form I've only seen him don once before, the one where he's half again as large with coal-black wings. Any trace of their normal jewel tones had vanished. Exhaustion spilled from him, but he'd keep going until he ran out of magic.

With me by his side—and the lines at our disposal—it would never happen.

The ley lines whispered through me. I listened and moved to the back of the host threatening Blake. Was any of this real? Or was it scene after scene on a never-ending tape loop rewinding and starting over endlessly?

Didn't matter.

I looped lines around the rear guard. Once I had a circle, it floated upward and cinched tight, choking life out of those I'd captured. One by one, they burst into noxious-smelling bundles of disconnected flesh.

My eyes widened. They'd never been alive to start with, merely constructs slapped together by the cowled one with the unnerving eyes. Laughter roared through me. Feeling like the wicked queen in *Alice in Wonderland*, I screeched, "Off with your heads," and turned the ley lines loose until the only one left standing was the dark lord—or whoever he was.

I danced across the ghost chamber jumping burning piles of what was left of the imaginary army. When I got close to Blake—who still hadn't acknowledged my presence—I stood between him and the hooded figure.

"Show yourself," I bellowed.

The lines chose that moment to come to life around me in a macabre magical ballet.

Terrifying laughter burst from the monster. "Remember, little one, you asked." He tossed the hood aside and opened his arms. Damn all the worlds, I wanted to walk into them. He was beauty incarnate, everything any man should be, with shiny dark hair falling in waves to his waist. Turquoise eyes were set in a magnificent face with sculpted cheekbones, a high forehead, and a square chin. Had the red eyes been a reverse glamour?

Next, he let the robe slip from his shoulders. His skin gleamed golden in the semi-darkness. He was tall, stately, with perfectly muscled shoulders, arms, and legs. A tantalizing phallus rose from its nest of spiky black hair, perfectly formed, perfectly huge, perfectly hard.

My mouth went dry. Heat and need pounded through me. Consequences be damned, I had to have him.

"That's right," he purred. "You were made for me long ago. The Celts realized their error and tried to hide you away. They cast a spell that forbade me from hunting for you, but you finally found me. I knew you would, eventually.

"Their enchantment no longer applies. Come to me, darling. We will rule as king and queen of everything. Nothing in this world or any other will be able to stand against our combined power."

Blue-green eyes bored a hole clear through into my soul. I took a step forward, and then one more.

"That's it," he crooned. "Once I can touch you, we shall become one."

A battle raged in my head. I tried to turn around to anchor myself by looking at Blake, but I couldn't move in any direction other than toward my nemesis. His lips parted displaying fangs.

"Vampire." The word ripped from me.

That laugh bathed me again; this time it wasn't as scary. Aw crap, I was sinking. "That and so much more," he agreed jauntily. "No secrets shall stand between us once you are mine." He stroked his phallus and thrust his hips miming sex.

The ley lines had turned quiescent, as if they were waiting for something from me. I heard Arianrhod's voice but couldn't make out her words.

My right foot rose, intent on closing the short distance

between me and my destiny. I shut my eyes, wrangled them closed. It was the only path to sanity. Never mind what I wanted. None of this was real. Compulsion streamed from my enemy.

Why hadn't I recognized it before?

The ground undulated beneath my feet pushing me closer to the lines. Reaching for the nearest ones, I grabbed them and shrieked, "Help me." Magic spilled into me like a bucket of ice water mingled with a series of electric shocks. I opened my eyes in time to see the lines take action.

Like a pack of snakes, they surged forward and wrapped themselves around the vampire—or whatever he was. He changed before my eyes, shifting into an eagle, then a serpent, and finally a shiny black dragon.

Before he vanished, absorbed by the lines, I heard, "We could have had it all, you stupid, stupid fool."

"Not so stupid as all that," I gritted. My body was still on fire with unnatural heat, but it would fade. I ran to Blake. No longer on his feet, he knelt on the red dirt, a glazed look on his face.

Their work done, the lines regrouped, circling around us. "Thank you," I told them without groveling or going into details about how close I'd come to making a mistake I'd never have recovered from. Once the shapeshifting bastard had me in his clutches, I'd have been his slave forevermore. He'd left that niggling part out in his rosy predictions about our wonderful future.

How could I have been so gullible?

Later. I'd sort everything out later. For now, I beckoned

to the lines and had them circle Blake, breathing magic and healing into his prostrate form.

Bit by bit, the lines and I drove darkness from his mind. It had quite a toehold. In a distant corner of my consciousness, I heard Arianrhod tell me I had this just before she took on a pack of wolf-things intent on annihilating us.

By now, I saw through a two-sided mirror. Blake and I were on one side, the battle on the other.

"Abria?" His voice was raspy, rusty, as if he hadn't used it in years.

"Yes, dear one. I'm here. Welcome back." Angling my head, I kissed him full on the mouth.

"What happened?" he murmured once I broke our kiss. "You were walking toward the vampire, and then everything is hazy."

"I'll tell you later. The others need us. Do you feel up to it?"

He nodded and staggered to his feet with the help of me and the lines. When we released him, he shook himself and smiled crookedly, looking like the Blake I used to know.

From the sounds of things, the battle was winding down. Made sense since the ley lines had conquered the one in charge.

"I have an idea," I told Blake. "Want to help?"

His smile bloomed full tilt. "How could I say no? I owe you my life."

"Not the whole story. I owe you mine right back." One more kiss, and I continued. "Let's free the animals. Someone conscripted them and then turned them into monsters."

Herne galloped close. I started to chant, weaving power between my hands.

Blake joined me. After a surprised sounding bellow, Herne did as well.

Power cascaded through the caverns touching animals as they passed through its vortex.

Would this work? I had no idea, but if any beast had a shred of its old self still present in the collection of misshapen bodies we'd fought, I could piece it back together, make it whole.

"Brilliant," Ceridwen shouted and joined us.

Odin pelted over and slung a war axe into the ground. "This is ridiculous," he brayed. "We won. Time for mead and celebration."

"No one wins unless we all do." I broke off chanting long enough to send a pointed glance his way.

The ravens, Huginn and Muninn, flew close. Rather than Odin, they landed on my shoulders. Aho! Guess whose side they were on this time.

Amidst Odin's grumbling, I renewed my chant. This time many voices joined their magic with my efforts. Once Becca cantered over, I began to hope I might win more than my personal battle with the dark lord.

When you cut to the chase, I'm an animal mage. It was what I was born for, the place I feel most fulfilled. If I could salvage even a few of these poor bastards, it would make everything we'd suffered today worthwhile.

Hedrek flew out of nowhere, hooting and cooing as he chucked his power into my efforts.

Blake stood proud by my side, augmenting my magic with his own.

Birgit slung an arm around my shoulders and added her considerable witchy power to the mix. Jethro rubbed my shins purring up a storm.

I'd come mightily close to throwing everything away. A shiver rippled through me, and then one more.

Might-have-beens don't matter, I reminded myself. A million promises to be more careful wouldn't mean a twit. *Careful* would mean I wasn't me. I wrapped a hand around a nearby ley line. They'd be with me always. Them and Blake and my animals. My heart cracked wide open; love poured out weaving into my casting as I called my children back from the horrors they'd endured.

I couldn't save them all, but we'd free their spirits. No one from today's battle would be consigned to one more second as a puppet for dark forces.

A lofty goal, but may as well aim high.

"I love you," Blake murmured next to my ear.

Cuddling closer, we blended Sidhe and Celtic magics. They took wing, beating back the last vestiges of evil.

CHAPTER 18

BLAKE

I remembered cutting the head off the spear and pulling the parts out of me. Arianrhod screeching in my ear was another highlight as I cursed myself for not moving faster. If I hadn't been so intent on killing, I'd have noticed the spear and twirled out of its path. I'd been warded. I still couldn't wrap my head around how the spear had defeated my protections.

I'd been fighting animals. A spear was the last thing I expected.

Excuses. Excuses...

Everything grew cloudy after that until I woke in the midst of a battlefield. Disturbingly familiar to the one the Celts had staged for me, it ebbed and flowed with bizarre animals charging but never getting too close. A robed figure seemed to be manipulating the puppet strings, but he never actually threatened me, either.

My mind was mush, so it took a while for the obvious to sink in.

I was naught more than bait. Finally, the spear made sense. He'd wielded it, not one of the animal host. The cowled mage didn't want me, though. If I was his primary goal, he'd have done something other than plop me in the midst of what felt more and more like an illusion.

My money was on Abria. She'd come after me, and then he'd pounce. I really, really wanted to be wrong about that.

But I wasn't.

Worse, I couldn't talk to Abria when she did show up, couldn't so much as flicker an eyelid. By now, I'd figured out who the wicked one was. I'd never met him before, but I'd come across him in lore books so old the vellum crumpled beneath my fingertips no matter how carefully I unrolled the scrolls.

When every world was in its infancy, a mage lusted after dragon magic. He planned and plotted and was nearly killed during his first several attempts to divest a dragon of its power center. After that, he laid low for a while and must have learned something because he made the transition to vampire before trying again.

Fangs and vampiric mesmerism were enough to skew the odds in his favor. To be fair, mesmerism had to be the key to his eventual success. He picked a young dragon, which helped. Lured the youngster with promises of endless gold to pad his hoard. When the eager dragon flew to the appointed place, a trap snapped shut.

The mage planned well. The snare was situated near magnetic plates that deflected attempts at long-distance communication. To be on the safe side, in case he'd miscalculated, the mage put distance between himself and the captive dragon. And he stayed gone a good long time. Had another dragon come across the unfortunate one, the mage would have disavowed all knowledge, but he never had to deal with that development.

No one came looking for the missing dragon.

After a hundred years with no food or water, the youngling was so feeble, the mage strolled in, chopped out the portion he wanted—scales and all—and freed the dragon. Of course, by then the creature was too weak to fly. No one knows what happened to him, but I always felt sorry for the youngling. Separated from home and hearth, perhaps he died of a broken heart.

Shame could have killed him too, but it's neither here nor there.

Funny what goes through your head when you're helpless. After Abria found me, things went from bad to worse. The dark mage turned up the juice, made himself irresistible.

Had he always possessed such a godlike visage and body? Impossible to know since vampires acquire an unholy beauty after they're turned. I always assumed it was to make it simpler to lure mortals to twist their necks in surrender, but I've never dug too deeply into that pit.

The undead disgusted me with everything from their feeding habits to their seethe structure. Master vampires establish dominion with sex and blood. Once they grow old enough, a few can actually fly and wield primitive magic.

Not so primitive. He'd caught me with almost zero effort.

Humility is a bitter pill, but this wasn't a beach I was willing to die on. When my mind was my own, I tried everything I could think of. Fire. Air. Torrents of water. As soon as anything I ginned up got close to doing some good, the mage pulled the shovel out of my hands, and I was back wandering through an opaque mist.

Maybe I'd only imagined manipulating the elements. It was a strong possibility none of this—except my captivity—existed other than inside my head.

Fuck me. I tried to break free. Every effort met with failure. I reached for a ley line, but they weren't close enough. Besides, they didn't answer to me.

Abria was moving nearer the mage. She didn't want to heed his call, but she was having one hell of a time resisting. *"Help her,"* I urged the lines. My telepathy was weak, but maybe they heard me since they slithered closer to her.

I tried to push telepathy Abria's way, but couldn't. The mage did not want me communicating with her. He knew about our connection, and his goal was to sever it.

No longer sluggish, my mind flitted from this solution to that. I reached deep, called to Earth, and begged her to intervene. The ground heaved and rolled. It pushed Abria into a ley line. She made a grab for it and came to her senses.

If I'd had a voice, I'd have whooped and hollered and screamed. All that noise reverberated inside but never made it out my mouth. Between the lines and Abria shutting her eyes for a moment, she broke the thing's hold over her.

It didn't go quietly. Before it finished shapeshifting, it

doused me in evil so pervasive I wanted to gouge my eyes out. The lines wound around him as he flitted from shape to shape, squeezing tighter every time. The chamber flooded with light so bright my eyes ached. When it cleared, both them and the mage were gone. Unbelievably, the battle playing out in my mind still raged. If the mage was behind it, it should be gone too.

Abria turned her full attention on me. The feel of her power was sweet, and I quit struggling to sort out why the battle hadn't disintegrated to dust. I tried my damnedest to help, but it took a long time for her and the ley lines to call me back.

A long time before I was more than dead weight.

I sucked purifying breath after purifying breath. I'd thought the lines were gone, but two pulsed next to us, circling me with cleansing light.

"Abria." My voice was barely there.

"Yes, dear one. I'm here. Welcome back." She bent and kissed me once, hard and deep. I sensed how worried she'd been, how close she'd come to being sucked into the mage's insidious enchantment.

"What happened?" I murmured once she broke our kiss. "You were walking toward the vampire, and then everything is hazy."

"I'll tell you later. The others need us. Do you feel up to it?"

I nodded and lurched to my feet. Once Abria let go, I shook myself from head to toe to reclaim who I am. Evil carves a deep path in a man. I needed to stand in hot water and let it run down my body until I felt clean, but it would have to wait.

From the sounds of things, the battle was winding down. Made sense since the ley lines had conquered the one in charge.

"I have an idea," Abria said. "Want to help?"

I grinned. "How could I say no? I owe you my life."

"Not the whole story. I owe you mine right back." She kissed me again. I held her tight, never wanting to let go.

"Let's free the animals," Abria murmured. "Someone conscripted them and then turned them into monsters."

"Of course. I'll help any way I can."

No rest for any of us. I managed one more quick kiss, reveling in the press of her lips against mine. It reminded me how narrowly I'd escaped. If the mage had nabbed Abria, I'd have become as much of an anachronism as the dragon he'd stolen magic from.

The battle was winding down, but we had yet to win the war. After grabbing my hand, she sprinted across the chamber heading for the others.

Without warning, we were back in the thick of things. She was determined to salvage as many animals as she could. They'd been through hell, their bodies distorted and deformed.

When summoned, my power roared back to life. I joined my enchantment with hers determined to support my love any way I could. Besides, the animals savaged by the dark mage deserved so much more.

Soon, Odin's contingent, the unicorns, the Sidhe, and Herne joined us. Hedrek too, and Odin's ravens.

We worked toward a common goal.

The desolate place we'd waged war took on spots of color. Earth was cleansing this spot of taint. Never mind we weren't on Earth. Gods and goddesses go where they're needed.

In this instance, Earth had heeded my earlier call. So long as she was here, she identified wreckage requiring her special touch.

Ceridwen set up shop in front of her cauldron reconnecting rightful parts of animals. I'd thought the bizarre creatures resulted from gene splicing or some other laboratory manipulation. It had been far more primitive. Someone —probably the vampiric mage—had chopped animals into bits and glued parts together with magic to please his horrific sense of humor.

With him gone, the animals dissolved into pieces. Figuring out which elements went together was the toughest part. Some were too far gone to heal, but we salvaged over half of them.

After an initial spate of grumbling, Odin was helpful. So were Hel and her serpents. Abria led us in a chant to focus and join our magic as we fed it into each damaged beast.

Arianrhod sidled next to me. "You gave me quite a scare, Sidhe."

I grinned her way. "Not much fun for me, either."

"What happened in the place you traveled?"

Interesting. She didn't know, or she wouldn't have asked. "The dark mage wanted Abria. I was bait. She figured it out, called the ley lines to assist, and the rest was history." I dusted my hands together.

"Pfft. He didn't want her. He wanted the ley lines." The

goddess screwed her face into a scowl. "If he'd have gotten his grimy paws on them, it would have been the end of magic for the rest of us."

"Oh, so you remember him?" I arched a brow.

"Better than you," she retorted. "He tried his phony seduction routine on me millennia ago."

"He's gone for good."

"How can you know?" the goddess asked.

"The ley lines incorporated him. They'll bleach his evil and turn it into more enchantment for the rest of us."

"Hope you're right about that."

"Ask Abria. She'll know."

"Maybe I'll do that." Arianrhod turned away and walked toward where Ceridwen, Birgit, and Abria were sorting body parts.

Breanne and Kirwan plodded close. "Quite a day." Breanne sounded pleased. Her axe was strapped across her back, its blade coated with dried blood.

"Aye," Kirwan spoke up. "The Sidhe haven't gone to war in over five hundred years."

"We're out of practice." Breanne tossed her head back.

"What would you do to correct that lapse?" I asked.

She settled hands on her broad hips. "Oh, so now you're finally ready to listen?"

I winced at the reminder. Before she got lost in I-told-you-sos, I said, "Would you do me the honor of heading up our army?"

Her normally dour expression flowed into a smile. "Thought you'd never ask."

"I'm not planning on any more battles—" I began.

"You didn't plan on this one. Or the earlier one in Rait Castle's courtyard. Better prepared than not," she cut in and pounded Kirwan across the shoulder blades. "You'll help me get this organized."

"But I'm more the academic sort," he sputtered.

I beat back a grin as they walked away deep in conversation about how to best fortify our defenses. We'd become complacent. Underhill did most of our dirty work for us, not allowing enemies to enter in the first place.

All fine and well, except we had to leave sometime. And when we did, we were vulnerable to whatever wicked forces had targeted us whilst we were concealed behind age-old spells.

The dark mage wasn't the only spot of evil in the lore books. Despite my assurances to Arianrhod, I wasn't at all certain he was gone for good. Old and wily, he'd survived worse than what we dished out today.

What happened next with him would be up to the ley lines. If they were patient, they could truly strip him of the power that made him dangerous. But if he was too big a thorn in their hide, they might dump him in a pit and assume he'd never escape.

Vampires are immortal. They can exist for long periods of time without sustenance. It made him exceedingly dangerous, but I trusted the ley lines knew all that and more.

I'd just taken up the healing chant again when Cailleach joined me. "Glad you made it through in one piece, Sidhe. I've grown fond of you."

"I tend to grow on people," I told her with a deadpan expression.

She punched me, but not especially hard. "What's next?" she asked.

It was an odd question given we'd be heading back soon. "What do you mean?" I assumed business as usual, but perhaps the witch goddess was privy to additional information.

"If Ceridwen is to be believed, your daughter will grow to become a Sidhe queen. Those eager for your downfall will target her."

"Not for a very long time," I protested. "By then, she'll have grown into her magic, and—"

Cailleach leaned close. "Listen to yourself. The child will have enemies, and they understand she'll be simpler to dispatch before she attains her full power."

"Other than the Cait, I didn't believe we had any true adversaries," I muttered.

"Think again," she snapped. "Others have lusted after your share of the magical pie for as long as I've been alive."

Before I could mine for details, she melted into the crowd.

I joined Abria, and we spent the next span of time resurrecting animals. The ones beyond hope were at least whole again, their spirits free to roam the halls of their ancestors.

Herne bellowed—his way of requesting our attention.

We were just finishing with the last group of animals, so his timing was good. I held out a hand and hauled Abria to her feet. We joined the group circled around the horned god.

By some small miracle, Odin and his band were still

here. He'd been threatening to leave since we dispatched the dark mage. Typical. He'd wanted to see this through for the glory, for bragging rights. Helping wounded animals to recapture wholeness probably wasn't high on his to-do list.

"Today had to happen," Herne began. "It was foretold many times over. No matter which prophecy I consulted, I saw the same events." He paused and huffed out a breath. "What was hidden from me was the outcome. I am relieved our losses were so few."

He pranced closer to Odin. "I would take up my position as head of my Wild Hunt. There is room in the skies for us both."

I expected Odin to scoff and tell Herne to beat it. Instead, the Norseman nodded. "Aye, that there is. I will not capture you again." He held out a ham-sized hand. Herne raised a hoof and bumped it into Odin's open palm.

The stag turned to the rest of us. "Thank you for believing in me enough to make today happen."

"What would you have done if we hadn't?" Arianrhod asked.

Herne shook his antlers. "I'd have gone alone. As I said, today was foretold. Had I been by myself, I would have failed."

"But you said the outcome was hidden," Arianrhod reminded him.

"Aye, but you saw what we faced. I'm powerful, but I am only one. Had you not been here, I'd have been swept away by a tide of wickedness."

An up-close-and-personal sensation of exactly what that tide had felt like lingered, and I agreed with him.

He bowed his head, clearly done for now.

I stepped to his side and augmented my voice with magic. "Please. Come to Underhill. I shall open its doors to one and all. We shall feast, and our bards will memorialize this day's victory with song."

No one waited for a second invitation. Mages left the killing field in small groups. Abria crouched over the last batch of animals ensuring their transition was complete. Once they were whole, she returned them to their homes with a magical assist. I looked for where I could help, but she had things well in hand.

After rising, she stood by my side, and I asked, "Ready?"

She nodded. Dark circles scribed beneath her eyes. Dirt was smeared across her face and up her hands to her wrists. "I'd like to sleep for a week, but I can do that after we celebrate."

Protectiveness spilled through me. For her and our unborn babe. "You can rest, love. The celebration will go on for days."

Her beautiful mouth curved into a soft smile. "Take us back. I'll be good once I've cleaned up."

I closed my arms around her, summoned power, and held a vision of Underhill. When we got near, its magic would guide us home. I instructed the Faery kingdom to allow all from the battle to enter unchallenged.

The return trip didn't seem to take as long. Abria fell asleep leaning against me. Safe in our chamber, I carried her to the bed, lay next to her, and kept watch while she slept.

We'd join the festivities soon enough.

"Blake." Her voice was saturated with fatigue.

"Aye, darling."

"Half an hour. Don't let me sleep a moment longer."

I must have hesitated because she pressed, "Promise."

"Anything." I kissed her forehead, her cheeks, and her lips before setting a mental alarm to make certain I held true to my word.

CHAPTER 19
ABRIA

I was who woke us, but I couldn't find it in me to chide Blake. I studied him slumbering next to me. Exhaustion had carved new lines in his perfect features. I scanned him with my power, but gently. A few shadows lurked in the corners of his psyche, but they were fading.

Of the two of us, he'd trod a far more difficult road. The dark mage, whose name I still didn't know, had played his hand well.

What he hadn't counted on was the extent of my magic—or my link with the ley lines. Embarrassment rolled through me. I'd nearly fallen for the oldest trick in the book. The fucker hadn't been the least bit interested in me. Nope. He'd wanted the ley lines and made the assumption I'd bring them with me to our bed.

Wherever he'd been keeping himself these past half dozen centuries, it had to be a world where women still kowtowed to men.

I had no idea how much time had elapsed since I fell on my face and passed out, but if we didn't light a fire under things, Blake's people would show up pounding on the door.

Wrapped in arms and wings, I tried my best to extricate myself without disturbing Blake but had little luck. He just held on tighter.

"Blake, sweetheart. We need to get up. Let me go and I'll get the shower going."

Dark eyes flew open. "Ach. I'm sorry. I meant to wake us, but—"

I placed a finger over his mouth. "It's all right."

Since I no longer had to be careful, I slithered from his various appendages and trotted across to the bathroom. Gleaming marble damn near blinded me as I debated between a soak and a shower.

The shower won since it wouldn't take as long. I was mostly soaped and shampooed when Blake joined me, sinking his hands into my soapy hair. I rubbed lavender-scented soap on his body, but touching him was always a slippery slope.

We'd already played hooky napping.

Between us, his cock rose to fullness. I soaped it too but shook a finger in his face. "Later. Your people need you more than me."

"Is that so?" Angling a showerhead, he doused me with water.

Several spigots lined the marble wall. Two could play that game, so I turned another on and aimed it his way. By the time we were clean, we were giggling like a couple of five-year-olds.

I shut the water off and tossed a towel his way. Rather than wrapping it around his waist, he chucked it over his shoulders and ran a hand up his shaft, the invitation all too clear.

"No one should be as irresistible as you," I told him and skirted past on my way to find something to wear.

"Not irresistible enough," he teased as he joined me in the bedroom.

Anything I had to wear that was remotely festive was at my flat in Nairn. "Um, where are all those clothes you keep lying around?"

"The wardrobe room?"

I nodded.

"One floor down, and to the northeast. Underhill will guide you."

The same way they guided me to the kitchens...

Maybe now that I was pregnant, the Faery domicile would be more supportive of consistently finding nourishment for me. I'd ordered up a thing or two, but it didn't mean future efforts would meet with equal success.

I draped a robe around myself. "Where shall I meet you?"

A smile started in his eyes and spread to his mouth. I swear, he is the most beautiful, the most perfect man I've ever laid eyes on. "Use your magic," he suggested. "I'm never far away."

I longed to throw myself into his arms. He was still buck naked, phallus curved tall and proud against his stomach.

He must have tuned into my inner struggle because he winked broadly.

Before I weakened, I hurried through the apartment and on out the door. Distant sounds of revelry met my ears, but I couldn't show up in a bathrobe. A flight of stairs leading down materialized off to my right. I took it and opened my essence to Underhill.

This time, it led me to a large room outfitted with chests, cupboards, and shelves. Someone had gone to a great deal of trouble arranging garments. Men's were on one side, women's on the other. Clothing from ancient to modern presented itself, and most everything I tried on fitted.

After debating, I settled on a formfitting sky-blue gown with long sleeves that were puffy at the shoulder and fitted at the wrist. A mirror and stand appeared, along with brushes and jeweled combs. I wrestled my hair into a semblance of order and held it in place with the combs. All I needed was a pair of sandals and perhaps a necklace.

The shoes were simple enough to locate, but if there was a hidey-hole for jewelry in this room, I couldn't find it.

A muffled snort blew past my lips. Perhaps Underhill didn't believe I needed adornment. Remembering myself, I bowed low and murmured, "Thank you for the borrowed finery. And for making it simple to find."

A gentle hum filled the air. Intriguing. Underhill truly was sentient, another manifestation of magic not unlike the ley lines.

I'd tarried long enough. Head held high, I walked out of the wardrobe room and up a convenient set of stairs. From there, I didn't need magic. I followed the sounds of music and laughter and the delectable scents of food.

My stomach gurgled, reminding me I hadn't eaten in a while. No more skipping meals, not while I was feeding two.

A few twists and turns brought me to the foyer outside the council chamber. Doors on several sides were propped open, and the council chamber looked larger.

"There she is," Herne boomed and clopped over to me. "A toast to Abria."

My name, *slainte*, and various other Gaelic toasts swirled. Heat crept up from the suddenly too-low neck of my gown, suffused my face, and washed over the top of my head.

I felt Blake's unique magical signature as he hurried toward me. When he was about three meters away, he stopped dead and stared.

Had I done something wrong? Was this some distant relative's special dress? Had I trespassed by borrowing it?

Before I could stammer excuses and offer to change, he closed the distance between us. "You are so beautiful. You take my breath away." Bending, he settled his mouth on mine and circled arms and wings around me.

Nearby people cheered. Distant groups took up the chant. When it changed from my name to queen, I wriggled out of Blake's arms. I tried to correct them, but my voice was swept away in a tide of others.

Finally, I jumped on a nearby table and cheated by using magic to silence the throng. When I had their attention, I said, "Thank all of you for your confidence in me, but I am Blake's mate, not your queen."

Arianrhod appeared next to me. She'd changed into a blood-red robe sashed in white. "Abria speaks true," she told the crowd.

Ceridwen plopped down next to the other goddess. Her robe was cream colored sashed in indigo. The kettle crashed to the ground next to her. Much to my surprise, she joined me on my perch and laid a hand over my belly.

Her touch was hot and prickly as she connected with the life within me.

Ceridwen's normally somber expression dissolved in smiles. "I had to check," she informed everyone. "The child is, indeed, a girl. She will be your queen, and her name shall be Tiana."

"You do not get to name her," I said, keeping my voice hopefully low enough no one else would hear.

Ceridwen had moved her hand from my belly. She patted my shoulder. "I did not name her. She told me her name when I looked within."

I may have mumbled something like, "We'll see about that."

Today was for celebrating, not for arguments. If I had to duke it out later with Ceridwen, I would.

Birgit hurried over, offering heartfelt congratulations. "Jethro says he can't wait to scry the child's future," she murmured.

"Be sure and tell me everything," I said.

"When you visit—and do make it soon—we'll have a nice cuppa, and I'll do just that." The witch smiled.

I grinned back. "We have a deal."

After lowering myself to a sit, I got off the table and

joined Blake. Time passed in a rush as we ate, drank, and accepted congratulations. The mead was strong and plentiful. Some curled up in corners to sleep off its effects.

After razzing Blake about getting the woman who should have been his, Odin rounded up his crew and left for Asgard.

Becca clopped up with Hedrek on her back. "Feel like a ride?" she asked.

I wouldn't have thought of it without her saying so, but it felt like a solid suggestion, so I jumped astride her broad back.

"Any chance I can come along?" Blake asked.

A black unicorn joined us and said, "Hop on."

We trotted along Underhill's passageways and through a wall. Magic shimmered around us until the Rait Castle courtyard took shape from the murk of our journey channel.

It was night on Earth. Deep, dusky, velvety. Some point past midnight, which lessened our odds of running into anyone. Still, the unicorns blocked out their horns, and Blake adopted his human glamour sans wings.

A shawl would have been welcome, but the night wasn't overly chilly by Scottish standards. Air swooshed above our heads from two directions as both versions of the Hunt traveled the skies.

"I wondered if Herne was going to stick around," I murmured.

"He and I talked about that very thing," Blake said. "He is always welcome in Underhill, but he said he was searching for a spot to call home where he and his huntsmen can abide in harmony."

I sent love and hope out into the universe. He'd been a captive for far too long. He deserved peace and happiness. Besides, I wanted an opportunity to get to know him better. We were linked through my dreams. Maybe someday, I'd even take to the skies with his Hunt.

The thought made me laugh.

"What's so funny?" Becca asked.

I shrugged. "I was imagining being part of Herne's Hunt, and then it occurred to me there are no women."

"You can be the first," Blake said.

"On a more serious note," I murmured, "what happens now?"

"What do you want to happen?" The other unicorn spoke up.

"After I've slept for a week and eaten everything in front of me?"

"Aye, after you've recovered," the unicorn whinnied.

I thought about it. Part of me had sort of assumed I'd return to my private detective business, but it wasn't going to happen. I wasn't all that interested in it anymore, for one thing. For another, I had bigger irons in the fire than helping mortals out of messes they'd landed in because of their own stupidity.

"I want to get to know the Sidhe," I said slowly. "Truly know them and determine how I fit into Underhill and their lives." I glanced at Blake. "Your turn."

"I've been thinking about that," he said. "I plan to shore up the council structure, redo our statutes, and forge an alliance with Odin. We've been on the outs forever. Time to mend that bridge."

"The child will need her place clarified before her birth," Becca said.

"Aye," the other unicorn added. "She must be the Sidhe queen memorialized in legends, and such shall be made clear before her birth."

We walked on through the darkened countryside for another half hour before we reached an ancient circle of standing stones. We weren't here by accident. The unicorns had something in mind.

I slid down. Blake joined me on the ground. Together, we walked within the circle and joined hands. Earth magic surrounded us smelling of evergreens and damp soil.

The unicorns skirted the stones to join us. Without being told, I knew to grip Becca's horn with the hand not hanging onto Blake. He did the same with the black unicorn.

Something shifted. Colors swirled. Enchantment caught us in a cyclone. I felt my daughter's essence and Blake's and the unicorns'. And ever so much more. Cosmic forces surrounded us, guided us, nurtured us. Hope swelled we'd have a break before the next spate of bad guys jumped us from out of nowhere.

Yes. All would be well for a while. At least until Tiana was a few years old. I smiled. Now I was calling her by Ceridwen's name.

"No," a small voice insisted. *"It is my name."*

I started to laugh, and I was still laughing in fits and starts when the unicorns led us out of the sacred circle.

"Our daughter already has opinions," I murmured.

"Would you really want it any other way?" Becca whinnied.

Blake swept me into his arms. "She'll be perfect," he told me, "because she carries the blood of kings, queens, and the ley lines."

"Aye, perfect," Becca agreed. "Do you want to ride back?"

I glanced up at Blake. "Okay if we walk?"

"Anything, my love."

Becca nudged me with her horn. "See you soon. Let's go riding!"

After the unicorns vanished, I hooked my arm with Blake's, and we strolled through the velvety night. "It's how everything began," I reminded him.

"What do you mean?"

"I was riding Becca when you were so smitten by my charms, you flagged me down."

"I'm still smitten, wench."

This time, when he wound his arms around me, he crushed his mouth over mine. When I opened my eyes, we were back in Underhill next to our bed. "Convenient," I teased.

"Why have magic if you don't use it? Turn around."

"Why?"

"That dress has a million buttons. I'd like to get started on them."

Laughter rolled through me. I'd been laughing a lot lately, and it felt damned good. As the silk slid from my body, I twisted to face Blake and returned the favor by removing studs from his fancy shirt.

This might not have been the life the Celts planned for me—or maybe it was. In a few days or months or years— after I came up for air—I just might ask one of them. For now, Blake was my world. His hands, his lips, his body. Surrendering to urgency sweeping through me, I pushed him onto the bed. I'd worry about the rest of his clothes later.

Much later.

You've reached the end of *Salvaged*. When I initially built this series in my mind, it had three books and a novella, but when Abria became pregnant, I knew I had to write a fourth book. Hold tight. *Tiana* will be along soon.

While it's fresh in your mind, please leave a review for *Salvaged*. They mean so much to authors, and only take a few moments of your time.

Read on for a sample from *Tiana*, next of the Wayward Mage series.

BOOK DESCRIPTION: TIANA

I need more time to train Tiana, but our enemies won't wait for the young Sidhe Queen to embrace her full power.

At the drop of a hat—seemingly—I became a mother. Not that I'd ever considered the possibility of parenthood. If I had, whatever I came up with would have been far off the mark.

Tiana had opinions before she was born. Ones she was vocal about.

She inherited my affinity for animals, Blake's wings, and his Sidhe royal lineage. In Underhill, they hail her as their queen, which has made raising her far more difficult. If one of us says no, she runs to her bevy of honorary aunts and uncles, one of whom is sure to indulge her.

Between Tiana's magic and her position in Sidhe society, I assumed she'd be a target from the moment of her birth.

Somehow, a dozen years have passed. I've often let my guard down—and kicked myself for my lack of vigilance.

Steeped in magic, my wild child often gets lost in the moment. I need a few more years to entrain her power. But if I know that, so do our enemies. They will come for her.

When it happens, we must be ready. All of us.

TIANA, CHAPTER ONE, ABRIA

Twelve years after the end of the last book in this series.

I've gotten to know Underhill well since I took up residence here. Or maybe the magical land has gotten to know me. These kinds of things flow both ways. It took me a decade to finally let my flat in Nairn go. Blake was infinitely patient. He said I could keep it forever if it made me feel more secure, but I tired of adopting a glamour to make me appear as if I'd aged whenever I visited the place.

Since my sojourns—at least to my old flat—grew progressively fewer, I finally gave notice. My landlord was sorry to see me go. Of course, he was. I was likely one of a handful of long-term tenants who always paid the rent on time.

A sharp knock at the door was followed by it slamming against the stops as someone shoved it open. Irritation blazed a trail through me. Blake may head the Sidhe, but they afforded him little respect and less than no privacy.

I was dressed this time, a plus. Today's choice was a flowing silk skirt in muted teal and violet tones. I'd layered a white woolen tunic over it and donned sturdy brown leather boots. I've learned to put on the day's clothing the minute I waken, and I'd been up for a couple of hours.

So much for my leisurely tea and biscuit breakfast while I worked my way through a new scroll Blake had unearthed about my specific type of magic.

On my feet, I strode from the kitchen. Before I reached the living room, Breanne met me with Tiana in tow. The Sidhe warrior is as broad as she is tall. Her considerable bulk quivered with outrage, making the circle of white curls around her head bounce. Gray eyes zeroed in on me.

"Do you know where I found *your* daughter?" she demanded.

Rather than falling for the bait, I stared pointedly at Tiana. She glared back, defiance dripping from every cell. "You were supposed to meet Kirwan in the library for your studies," I noted.

"Ha!" Breanne snorted. "He alerted me she never showed, so I hunted her down."

Breath hissed through my clenched teeth. Why in the hell hadn't Kirwan told me Tiana was missing? How many years would it take before I was more than "the mage married to Blake?" Or Elwyn as many of his subjects preferred to call him.

"Do you have anything to say?" I asked my daughter.

A mulish expression marred her features, and she fluffed her wings preparatory to spreading them and flying away. I dropped a magical lasso over her black and indigo appendages and said, "You are not leaving."

"But I wasn't done," she whined.

Fuckity fuck. "Done with what?" I asked both of them.

"I found her in a wolf's den," Breanne growled. "Took gobs of magic to extricate her. Momma wolf wanted to rip into me."

Alarm bells ran down my back. "You didn't hurt her—"

Breanne cut me off midsentence and stabbed a beefy index finger dead center into my chest. "Of course, not. Sidhe are sworn to do no harm to the natural world. But today is a prime example of why Tiana lacks self-discipline. You taught her your magic first, rather than ours."

We'd had this discussion before—many times. I'd be damned if I'd argue with another mage in front of my child.

I latched onto Tiana's gaze. It was like looking at a miniature replica of me. She has the same long red hair, the same clear green eyes. I see Blake in her pronounced cheekbones and square chin, but she has my forehead. Womanhood is a ways distant yet.

Thank all the goddesses who've ever walked any world. Hormones will complicate everything. Today, she was in a wolf's den. Tomorrow, I might find her entertaining the Sidhe youth who trail after her like she's a bitch in heat.

I pushed *that* thought aside. Sex might be a problem, but it wasn't today's issue.

I dropped a hand on my daughter's shoulder. "Go to your room. Remain there until I come to escort you to Kiran's quarters."

"But I hate my lessons. They're stupid." She stamped a foot.

"Not negotiable. Go now." I added a magical push.

So did Breanne. Still grumbling, Tiana stomped toward the hall leading to our sleeping chambers. Her wings were still hobbled, and I'd keep them so for a while.

To be on the safe side, I shut the front door and sealed it against her leaving. Even absent wings, she could leverage teleport magic, so I closed off her room as well as soon as she was inside.

"You have to keep a closer eye on her—" Breanne sputtered.

I laid a finger over my lips. "Feel like a cup of tea?" I asked.

A surprised expression raised Breanne's white brows. When she nodded, I beckoned and led the way back to the kitchen. Once we were seated over mugs of fragrant mint and rosemary tea fortified with mead, I dropped a sound shield over us.

"The child has ears like a lynx," I said, exhaling loudly.

"If I wouldn't have found her, goddess knows what might have happened," Breanne muttered.

I trod carefully. The entire wolf pack would have laid down their lives for Tiana, but this wasn't the time to mention it. "I appreciate you looking out for her—" I began.

"Someone has to," she inserted acidly.

So much for trying to be nice. My temper has never been my strongest asset. I slapped a hand on the tabletop. "She has to develop common sense. She can't do that if I'm constantly riding herd on her."

"Doesn't appear to be working very well," Breanne observed.

I wanted to strangle her. Instead, I agreed, "It could be working better. And it would if the rest of you simply asked her if she'd run this, that, or the other thing past either Blake or me. If she lies, you'll know. If she says no, we're as close as mind speech. Ask us if she's allowed out of Underhill on her own. Or whatever she claims she has a right to do. We'll set you straight."

"She said you told her it was okay for her to visit the wolf den." Breanne glanced upward as if requesting divine intervention. "There are new pups. They fascinate her. When I arrived, she was mind-linking with them and suggesting they'd grow up to include her in their pack."

Like many of Tiana's assertions, this one held elements of truth. "I did tell her she could visit—so long as Blake or I went with her. By default, she's part of every animal pack, group, murder, flock. You name it."

"I see," Breanne muttered.

"As for the other part," I plowed on, "the one about her learning my side of magic before the Sidhe side. It's not true. Sidhe magic is complex, more difficult to entrain. Like most children, she picked the simple path, and since animals follow her as if she's the Pied Piper—"

"The who?"

"Never mind. It's a human fable about a boy with a magical pipe."

"I see."

She didn't since she didn't know the tale, but it wasn't critical. "In any event, what child isn't fascinated by animals? They flock to her the same way they were drawn to me. Blake and I view it as harmless."

"Hmph. It is so long as she remains within Underhill's protections."

Finally, a point we agreed on. "Yes. True." I pressed my lips together. "Do you think she might do better with a different tutor?"

I expected outrage, but Breanne surprised me. "I've wondered the same. Kirwan was a solid choice for the odd youth we've produced, but he is getting on, and he's strict."

"Tiana needs strict," I mumbled.

"The way she behaves, she's a prime target." Breanne lowered her voice.

"Have you heard anything?" I demanded. Since I was still a second class citizen in Sidhe-land, I wasn't privy to much news unless Blake chose to share.

Breanne shook her head. "All is quiet. Too quiet if you ask me. In a few more years, Tiana will come into her full magic. No one will want to tangle with her then."

Our enemies had misjudged me—and rather badly. They could easily do the same with someone they considered a mere child, but I didn't give voice to that thought because it rattled me.

"Do you still post spies?" I asked.

Another surprised expression. "Doesn't Blake talk with you?"

I fought the same irritation that cropped up whenever the Sidhe closed ranks leaving me on the outside. "Sure, but not about everything."

"Aye, we have spies, but they can scarcely cover every

world." A hesitation before she added, "And we've had no luck posting anyone anywhere near Satan's realm."

"He wasn't who we fought last time," I reminded her.

"Others like the ancient vampire exist," she muttered darkly. "We can't keep tabs on them all."

"Don't get defensive." I set my cup down and refilled it, resettling the pot between us. She could pour her own tea if she wanted more.

"I wasn't. We need a better plan for your daughter."

"And your queen." I probably shouldn't have added that jab but couldn't help myself.

Blake chose that moment to walk into the kitchen. Because of the sound shield, I hadn't heard him enter our rooms. His mouth was moving, but of course I couldn't hear him.

No matter how many years we spend together, he still steals my breath. Tall and broad-shouldered, he has dark hair cut to shoulder level, penetrating dark eyes, a to-die-for facial structure, and gorgeous black wings with jewel-toned inserts. Today he wore black linen trousers and a western-style button down pale blue shirt with cutouts to accommodate his wings. Shiny black loafers peeked from beneath the trouser cuffs.

I held up a finger and reeled in my spell.

"Where is Tiana?" he demanded. "Kirwan told me she's missing."

"In her room," Breanne and I said in unison.

"Why can't I sense her?"

"Because I sealed her in there," I told him and girded

myself for a barrage of criticism. His baby, his princess, shouldn't be confined. Especially, not against her will.

Instead of censure, he asked, "Why?"

Breanne offered a decent encapsulation of the last hour.

He hooked a chair with his foot and plopped into it. After reaching for the teapot, he realized he didn't have a cup. I pushed mine in front of him. I was done, anyway.

"We need a better approach," he said and drained half a cup of the mead saturated beverage.

We sure did. What we'd been doing was an abysmal failure. "Mind if I haul her in here?" I glanced from Blake to Breanne.

"Why would you do that?" Breanne looked thunderstruck.

"If she's a part of decision-making that relates to her, maybe she'll be more compliant."

"Might work," Blake said and pushed to his feet.

I waggled a finger his way. "Uh-uh. I don't want you fussing over her or her whining about how badly she's been treated."

A corner of his mouth twitched; he reclaimed his chair while mumbling, "Guilty."

Reaching with magic, I removed the barrier around her room and told her, *"You will come to the kitchen now. If you deviate, you will be very sorry."*

"Oh? What would you do to me?" It's tough to project sarcasm along with telepathy, but she managed it.

Besides hang her upside down in a cave for a hundred years? Rather than reacting to her insolence, I said, *"You have thirty seconds to get your behind in here."*

On the thirty-first she sauntered through the kitchen doorway and stopped. I could see devious little wheels turning in her head as she made a beeline for Blake.

"Daddy. You're home." She tried to fling herself into his arms, but he didn't uncross them.

"I'm usually home," he commented and pointed to a fourth chair. "Sit down."

Her eyes widened. Usually Blake was the softest of soft touches.

"Don't make me tell you again." Steel sat behind his words.

Tiana walked around the table and sat in the indicated chair. She made a grab for the teapot.

"Put it down," I said. "You can have tea later, and not this batch."

"I've had mead before," she announced.

"Keep your mouth shut and listen," Breanne thundered.

Defiance bled out of Tiana's expression. She looked at the tabletop, waiting. Because I could, I delved into her thoughts and found confusion. Her take-no-prisoners attitude had always worked well for her. Why was it suddenly failing?

Breanne was glaring at Blake.

He got the picture. "Tiana, look at me," he commanded. Because it was punctuated with compulsion, she scraped her eyes upward and met her father's.

"Better," he said. "One day, you will be queen to your people. I have afforded you latitude because you're a child, but today's events convinced me your childhood should have ended long since."

"What does that mean?" she mumbled.

"For one thing, it means you will do what you're told. If you do not," he went on, "there will be consequences. Ones you find unpleasant. For starters, I will separate you from the animal mage part of your power if you ever repeat a stunt like the one you pulled today."

She was on her feet in a trice. "You can't do that," she shrilled and turned to me. "Momma. Tell him he can't do that."

I shouldn't have, but I couldn't help myself. I laughed. "You're appealing to me?" I got out in between bouts of mirth. "Talk about too little and too late, child."

Anger shot from her in hazy red waves. I neglected to mention she also inherited my temper. To her credit, she didn't say anything that would have sunk her deeper into Blake's bad graces.

So far, the ley lines had yet to accept her as my spawn. Wise of them. My bet was they were waiting for her to gain wisdom.

"From here on in," Blake was saying, "your days will be structured in the following manner. After breakfast, you will spend the morning hours with Kirwan learning about your Sidhe heritage and practicing that side of your magic."

"But he's boring," she protested.

Kirwan hustled into the kitchen on the heels of her words and shook a finger at her. "I heard that, youngling. Show some respect."

"Sorry," she mumbled.

"You can do that better," Blake told her.

Tiana got to her feet, bowed, and said, "I'm sorry. It won't happen again."

She wasn't the least bit sorry about anything beyond her freedom being curtailed, but at least she was able to pretend.

The old mage nodded. He's one of a handful who doesn't employ magic to hide his age. Wrinkles sat atop wrinkles giving him the appearance of a Shar-pei. A halo of silver hair circled his otherwise bald pate. His customary black robe was draped around his short, slight frame, and his feet were bare.

"Are you done with her?" he asked Blake.

"Not quite," Blake replied and stood to face his daughter. "Once your morning lessons are over, you will have luncheon. Then you will train with Breanne three days a week to learn how to fight."

Breanne cast a sidelong glance his way that said she'd rather host a pack of vipers, but he was her prince, so she didn't protest.

"Two afternoons a week will be spent with your mother honing your animal mage talent. The other two afternoons will be yours to choose, but you may never leave Underhill unaccompanied."

"What happens if I do?"

Aha. There was the daughter I'd come to know all too well.

"I will send you to Caer Sidi to spend at least a year with Arianrhod."

Tiana's eyes grew round. "You wouldn't."

"Och, aye, but I would. It's one place you can't escape from."

Tiana ran her palms down her black T-shirt embossed with runes and her black leather pants. For a kid who'd never been exposed to Western culture, she sure had a Goth bent.

For once, she'd run out of words.

Blake nodded at Kirwan. "She's ready for you. I want a report on each day's progress or lack thereof."

The old mage nodded sharply, crooked a finger Tiana's way, and stomped out of the kitchen.

After a short pause, Tiana followed him.

A sigh rattled through me once the front door opened and shut.

Blake closed his eyes for a moment, and then sat back at the table. After finishing off the mead-tea mixture, he said, "I hated to do that, but it was necessary."

His words caught my attention. "Why?"

"There is news," he said shortly. "Fell forces are mobilizing against us."

Breanne rubbed her big hands together. "Excellent. I'll call out our platoons, field them so they can sharpen their skills."

She moved fast for someone so large. It always surprised me. On her feet, she teleported out of the room.

Blake stared after her. "She didn't even wait to hear details."

"She might not have, but I need to know," I said. My mouth was dry; my stomach curled into a tight knot. I'd been waiting for this moment since before Tiana's birth. Now it was almost upon us, and fear gripped me.

We'd fight, but would it be enough?

Blake got up and hauled me to my feet. He wrapped his arms around me and held on tight. The show of affection—or was it desperation—wasn't making me feel any better.

"Out with it," I said, my words muffled against his shoulder.

"Come to our room," he replied. "I can shield it better than any other."

Our apartment isn't all that big, but it took several lifetimes to cover the distance from where we'd been sitting to our bedchamber. I waited while Blake shut the door and crafted a barrier around us, wanting to know and not at the same time.

When he finally turned to me, I blew out a breath I hadn't been aware I was holding and waited to discover the shape of my worst nightmares.

ABOUT THE AUTHOR

Ann Gimpel is a USA Today bestselling author. A lifelong aficionado of the unusual, she began writing speculative fiction a few years ago. Since then her short fiction has appeared in many webzines and anthologies. Her longer books run the gamut from urban fantasy to paranormal romance. Once upon a time, she nurtured clients. Now she nurtures dark, gritty fantasy stories that push hard against reality. When she's not writing, she's in the backcountry getting down and dirty with her camera. She's published over 100 books to date, with several more planned for 2022 and beyond. A husband, grown children, grandchildren, and wolf hybrids round out her family.

Keep up with her at www.anngimpel.com or http://anngimpel.blogspot.com

If you enjoyed what you read, get in line for special offers and pre-release special reads. Newsletter Signup!

ALSO BY ANN GIMPEL

SERIES

Alphas in the Wild

Hello Darkness

Alpine Attraction

A Run for Her Money

Fire Moon

Bitter Harvest

Deceived

Twisted

Abandoned

Betrayed

Redeemed

Cataclysm

Harsh Line

Warped Line

Cracked Line

Broken Line

Circle of Assassins

Shira

Quinn

Rhiana

Dragon Fury

Earth Reclaimed

Earth's Requiem

Earth's Blood

Earth's Hope

Elemental Witch

Timespell

Time's Curse

Time's Hostage

Gatekeeper

Shadow Reaper

Rebel Reaper

Untamed Reaper

GenTech Rebellion

Winning Glory

Honor Bound

Claiming Charity

Loving Hope

Keeping Faith

Ice Dragon

Feral Ice

Cursed Ice

Primal Ice

Magick and Misfits

Court of Rogues

Midnight Court

Court of the Fallen

Court of Destiny

Rubicon International

Garen

Lars

Soul Dance

Tarnished Beginnings

Tarnished Legacy

Tarnished Prophecy

Tarnished Journey

Soul Storm

Dark Prophecy

Dark Pursuit

Dark Promise

Underground Heat

Roman's Gold

Wolf Born

Blood Bond

Wayward Mage

Hands of Fate

Jinxed

Hunted

Salvaged

Tiana

Wolf Clan Shifters

Alice's Alphas

Megan's Mates

Sophie's Shifters

Wylde Magick

Gemstone

Lion's Lair

Unbalanced

STANDALONE BOOKS

Branded, That Old Black Magic Romance (paranormal romance)

Edge of Night (short story collection, paranormal and horror)

Grit is a 4-Letter Word (nonfiction)

Heart's Flame (post-apocalyptic romance)

Icy Passage (science fiction romance)

Marked by Fortune (post-apocalyptic coming of age story)

Melis's Gambit (historical paranormal romance)

Midnight Magic (paranormal romance)

Red Dawn (post-apocalyptic paranormal romance)

Shadow Play (historical paranormal romance)

Shadows in Time (Highland time travel romance)

Since We Fell (contemporary romance)

Warin's War (paranormal romance)